SATURDAY

E. L. Todd

Fallen Publishing

Saturday

CHAPTER ONE

Kyle

Honeycombs or Froot Loops?

Both had way too many carbs and sugar but I didn't care. A bowl of cereal once in a while wouldn't kill my eight pack. I glanced back and forth between them before I shoved both into the cart.

Oh well.

I walked further down the aisle and grabbed a carton of almond milk and a few bananas. Whenever I went grocery shopping, I only grabbed the essentials. If I bought too many things, they usually went to waste.

I moved down the next aisle and snatched a box of baking soda. That's when I noticed a familiar face, one I'd never forget. Her brown hair was longer than it used to be, reaching down to her waist. She still wore it the same way she always did, in a braid over one shoulder. While everything looked the same there was one obvious difference.

She was enormous.

"Frankie?" I tossed the baking soda into my cart then walked toward her. She was standing in front of the powdered sugar, probably looking for baking supplies.

When she turned around her face lit up like Christmas morning. She was happy to see me, over-the-moon. Not only did she smile with her lips, but her eyes showed the same joy. "Kyle?"

I looked down at her stomach, unable to believe what I was looking at. "Damn, you're about to pop."

Both of her hands moved to her swollen belly, and she chuckled like I gave her a compliment. "Yeah...I'm starting to get uncomfortable."

My eyes wouldn't leave her stomach. I was mesmerized by the life growing inside her. "You look absolutely stunning. Pregnancy suits you." Never in my life had I seen her look this happy. The glow that emitted around her was a beacon of light that the sun couldn't compete with. She still had a small frame so her stomach looked even bigger in comparison. "Congratulations."

"Thank you." She ran her hands along her belly, feeling the life inside. "Sometimes I can't believe there's a little person in there."

I came closer to her and extended my hand. "May I?"

"Of course."

I pressed my hand to the surface, noting the distinct hardness. There wasn't movement from within, but I could feel the warmth. "You must be due any day."

"Next week, actually," she said, still smiling.

I pulled my hand away and returned my look to her, seeing the joy permanently engraved on her features. She and I hadn't seen each other in a year, and now our old relationship seemed like a lifetime ago. She was about to bring a whole new person into the world. "Do you know what you're having?"

"A girl."

"Awe...little Frankie."

She continued to rub her belly. "Her name is Suzie."

"That's even cuter."

"Thank you. Hawke picked it out."

Saturday

The last time we spoke, she told me she was marrying Hawke. At the time, I was heartbroken, but now, I was happy. While I wanted her to end up with me, I knew in my heart she was meant for him. "He has good taste."

The mention of his name reminded her of the past. Flashbacks moved across her eyes, and then the guilt settled in. "Kyle—"

"I'm so happy for you." I didn't want her to feel bad about the decision she made. It was the right one. It took me months to come to that conclusion, and when I did, I felt better. "Truly."

Francesca knew me better than most people. It was easy for her to spot a lie and see the truth. Once she realized I meant every word I said, she smiled again. "How are you?"

"Great. My firm just won a big case, and I have a new apartment uptown."

"That's awesome."

"I'm not seeing anybody right now, but I was with this lawyer a while ago. She was cute and funny, but I broke it off when I didn't see it going anywhere."

"You'll find someone, Kyle."

I had no doubt that I would—someday. "Thanks."

"Well, a lot has happened this past year," she said. "I got married, got pregnant right away—"

"He didn't waste any time, huh?" I said with a chuckle.

She laughed. "Suzie was a mistake. But she's the best mistake either one of us made."

"I'm sure." I wanted kids someday. I always thought I would be a good dad, the kind that was around for everything. "I heard you opened another shop."

"I did," she said. "It's doing well."

"I figured." Francesca made everything come to life with her touch. She wasn't necessarily a great businesswoman, but she was a great people person. Everyone naturally gravitated toward her, wanting anything she could give.

Hawke rounded the corner than approached us down the aisle. He wore dark jeans and a gray t-shirt, a tattoo running down his left arm. A wedding band was on his left ring finger, black and noticeable against his fair skin. When he looked at me his features were stoic.

I wasn't Hawke's favorite person, and he wasn't mine either. He might punch me in the face if I didn't walk away right this second.

Saturday

He came to Francesca's side and stared me down, his thoughts still a mystery. He was naturally intense and rugged, infecting the air with hostility without actually doing anything. Then he did the unexpected.

He extended his hand to shake mine. "It's good to see you."

The gesture was so unexpected that I smiled. "You too." I shook his hand and returned it to my side. "Frankie was just telling me about the new addition to the family."

"Yeah, we're excited." He wrapped his arm around her waist. "I told her to stay home and rest, but she never listens to me...you know how that is." He stared at her fondly, like she was the only person in the room.

"I remember her being stubborn as hell, if that's what you're asking."

Frankie pressed her lips tightly together in a frown. "You're supposed to be sweet to pregnant women, not insult them."

"It wasn't an insult," I said.

"Yeah," Hawke said in agreement. "It was the truth."

She swatted his arm playfully. "Don't be a jerk."

E. L. Todd

"I'm your husband. It's part of my job description."

Francesca rolled her eyes.

Now that I said hello and took up enough of their time, I knew I should let them get back to whatever they were doing. "Well, it was great seeing you. Take it easy, okay?"

"I'm fine." She rubbed her stomach again before she stepped toward me. Then she turned her belly to the side and moved into my chest to hug me.

I hugged her back, my arms wrapped around her shoulders. "You're going to be a great mother, Frankie."

"You think so?"

"I know so." I rubbed her back gently before I let her go. "Just don't feed them too many muffins. They'll get addicted."

She chuckled. "I'll keep that in mind."

Hawke shook my hand again. "Take care, man." He didn't hunt me down with his eyes the way he used to. It was the first time he looked at me like I was a friend, someone he actually liked. Marriage must have changed his perspective on everything.

"You too. Congratulations."

"Thanks." He gave me a quick smile before he turned back to Francesca and wrapped his arm around her. He guided her down the aisle and to the cart parked off to the side.

I watched them walk away, feeling an inexplicable surge of joy shoot through me. Once upon a time, I loved that woman. She was all I ever thought about. I even bought an engagement ring because I was going to ask her to marry me. When it didn't work out, I was devastated and thought I would never be happy ever again. She was the one.

But I got through it.

I took it one day at a time until I stopped thinking about her altogether. All the grief and bitterness evaporated, and I was left in peace. Now I could watch her walk away from me without feeling an ounce of pain.

I was happy.

CHAPTER TWO

Kyle

I entered my office then plopped down into the chair. My role in the firm was mostly management. I oversaw the cases from a distance, and I took care of the paperwork and the payroll. When something really interesting came along, I jumped in feet first. Since that was rare, I usually just played golf all day.

My assistant spoke into my intercom. "Mark wants a word, sir."

"Don't call me sir." She was new so she didn't know how I ran things around here. "Kyle is fine."

"My apologies."

"Send him in."

"Will do."

Mark walked in a second later. "Hey, busy?"

Saturday

My feet were resting on the desk, and I was squeezing a stress ball. "Do I look busy?"

He dropped into the chair facing my desk and slid a folder across the mahogany wood. "I want your two cents about this case."

I opened the vanilla colored folder and searched through the brief. "I'm all ears."

"The judge dismissed the evidence because it was circumstantial. But they found the knife covered with the suspect's blood." He slammed his hand down on the desk. "Come on! How is that circumstantial?"

The law could be a fickle thing.

"I thought I had this fucker nailed to the wall, and then this happens. I swear, someone paid the judge off."

It wouldn't be the first time. "Give me an hour to look over this, and I'll get back to you."

"Thanks, man." When he rose to his feet he ran his fingers through his hair, pushing it back. "Let me know what you've got."

"Will do."

Mark walked out, and the second the door was shut my assistant spoke over the intercom again.

"Charles is here to see you, sir. I mean— Kyle."

"Charles who?" I knew a lot of people by that name.

"Charles Rubien."

My mother's boyfriend. I didn't realize he was stopping by today. "Send him in."

"Will do."

The doors opened again, and Charles walked inside. He wore a suit that was more expensive than a car, and his watch had more value than the average savings account. Despite his wealth he was humble—and that's why I liked him.

"Kyle." He extended his hand and shook mine vigorously. "It's nice to see you."

"You too. How are you?" Charles was a good guy. He was personable and warm, and he had a great sense of humor. But none of those things really mattered—including his wealth. He treated my mom right and made her happy. That was all I cared about.

"Great. I hope I'm not keeping you from anything." He took a look around my office, glancing at the pictures on the desk, before he turned back to me.

"The law never sleeps. That's nothing new." I sat behind my desk and placed the folder aside. "What's up?" He'd never come to my office before. My father opened this practice nearly thirty years ago, so it was still his in my eyes—even though he'd been done for nearly seven years now. To have my mother's boyfriend in his old office was a little strange. It was the first time it ever happened.

"Well, I wanted to talk to you about something. It may be a little uncomfortable for you, but I hope you take it well."

My eyes narrowed on his face because I had no idea what warning he was giving me. "You know I always have an open mind."

He adjusted his tie before he spoke. "Your mother is a wonderful addition to my life. After I lost my wife twelve years ago, I didn't think I'd ever fall in love again. Your mother is the perfect partner in every way possible, and I'd love to spend the rest of my life taking care of her. I hope I have your blessing before I ask her to be my wife."

My jaw dropped. "Say what?" I jumped to my feet and gripped my skull. "You're going to ask my mom to marry you?"

He chuckled and pulled the box out of his front pocket. "I am."

"No way."

"Way," he said with a laugh. He opened the box and displayed the enormous ring that contained more diamonds than it could handle.

I came around the desk to get a better look. "Damn, this will definitely make all the men steer clear."

"That's the point."

I examined the ring and watched every flawless diamond sparkle. It was made of white gold with a slender band. I didn't know much about jewelry until I bought Francesca's ring, but this suited my mom. "Dude, it's perfect."

"Thank you." He closed the box and returned it to his pocket.

It was weird to see Mom with another guy, but I knew it was time to move on. Dad had been gone for a long time, and he would want her to be happy. And I wanted her to be happy.

"So, you're okay with this?"

Charles was always nice to me, but he never crossed the line and tried to be anything more than my mom's boyfriend—which I appreciated. He understood he would never be a father figure to me because I didn't want him to be. "Absolutely."

He breathed a sigh of relief like he expected a different reaction. "I know this is hard. Thank you for being mature about it."

I shrugged. "I know my dad would want her to move on and be happy. And you're a great guy. Mom needs someone to look after her. When I settle down and have my own kids, I won't be around as much."

"Excellent points."

"So, when are you going to do it?"

"I'm taking her to Florence this weekend. I have a yacht there. When we're having dinner on the deck, I'm going to ask her."

"Damn, that's romantic as hell."

He laughed. "She loves Italy. It's her favorite place."

"She's definitely not going to say no to that."

"I hope so." He put his hands in his pockets and gave me a fond look. He seemed to genuinely like me, and not just because I was my mother's son. "You're a good man, Kyle. Your parents did a wonderful job raising you."

"Thanks. Mom is the best of the best."

He chuckled. "She is." He moved his hand to my shoulder and gave it an affectionate squeeze. "Wish me luck."

14

"With a yacht in Italy, you don't need any luck."

"I hope so."

"When I propose, you're going to have to give me some pointers."

He laughed as he headed to the door. "I have a feeling you don't need pointers from anyone, Kyle."

Saturday

CHAPTER THREE

Kyle

"Goddammit, Curry!" That was a clean shot, and he should have made it.

Will drank his beer. "Dude, everyone acts like he's the shit when he's not even that good. He can make a basket, big deal."

"He's scored more points than anyone else in NBA history." How could he sit there and say he wasn't that good? That was like saying Michael Jordan was just all right.

"Whatever." He sat beside me on the couch and set his bottle on the coffee table. "He's overrated."

"You're jealous."

"I'm jealous?" he asked. "Because I'm not an NBA player? Yeah…I guess I am jealous."

I grabbed a handful of the fries and devoured them. We ordered hot wings from this

17

place just a block away, and I had to make this meal my cheat for the week. But I didn't regret it because it was delicious. "Guess who I saw last week?"

"Le Bron?" he asked hopefully.

"No. I wish." I leaned back into the couch and rested my feet on the table. "Frankie."

Will was just about to take a drink of his beer when he stopped. "Frankie? The same Frankie you were going to propose to?"

I didn't talk about her much, especially with my friends. The months after we broke up were difficult, and it took me a long time to get back into the game. Dates were difficult, and sleeping around was nauseating. After I pushed through the worst of it, everything got better. "Yeah."

"Where?" He forgot about the TV and just looked at me.

"At the store. She was with Hawke."

"I'm sorry, man."

"No, I'm okay." I really was. Seeing her that happy made me happy. I didn't think I'd ever be able to get over her, but somehow I did. Now that relationship seemed like a lifetime ago. "She's pregnant. Like, she's about to pop."

"Really?"

18

"She's humongous—in a good way."

"Was it awkward?"

"No, actually." It was the first time I'd seen her in a year, but it wasn't tense like I imagined it would be. "It was nice. She seems happy, and I'm happy. It was a nice little moment."

"Good for you." He clanked his beer against mine. "I remember how hung up you were."

I shrugged. "I'll find the right girl someday—probably when the Victoria's Secret fashion show comes into town."

He chuckled. "I'm going to marry a model too—and not just for her looks."

"They can be our sugar mamas'."

"You're right about that." He clanked his beer against mine. "By the way, are you free on Friday night?"

I hated these types of questions. "It depends on why you're asking."

"A girl friend of mine from work set me up with someone. She wants me to do the same for her."

"Like, a blind date?"

"Yep."

I wasn't a big fan of blind dates, but I had nothing else to do on Friday night. "Sure. Why not?"

"Great."

"What's she like?"

"She's really smart. She works in the IT department—does a lot of coding."

"Is she cute?"

"Pretty cute."

That was all I needed. "Who's she bringing for you?"

"Not sure. One of her friends."

"Cool," I said. "Have you been going out a lot?"

"I met this girl at a Ranger game, and she was really cool. But it didn't work out."

"Why not?"

He shrugged. "She never called me back."

Rejection. Ouch. "Maybe you'll hit it off with this girl."

"Maybe," he said. "But she sounds shy, like she doesn't go out often. I'm not sure what to expect."

"Everyone is a little nervous on a blind date. I wouldn't worry about it."

"True."

We returned our focus to the game. Stephen Curry just made another three pointer before the fourth quarter ended. If he hadn't gotten that ball in the air just in time, the point wouldn't have counted.

Will clenched his jaw in irritation.

"He's awesome," I said. "There's no doubt about that."

Saturday

CHAPTER FOUR

Kyle

Will and I were already at the restaurant. It was an Italian place—fancy. I loved good food but didn't care for pretentious and expensive restaurants. The plates were always small, and they overcharged for everything. "What's my date's name?" I probably should have asked that sooner.

"Florence."

"Cool." My mom was in Florence at this very moment. Now I would have something to talk about with my date. "What's yours?"

"Rose."

"Cool." I eyed my watch. "When are they going to be here?"

He shrugged. "Aren't women always late?"

"Beats me."

Ten minutes later they walked inside. I assumed it was them because they were alone and searching the restaurant.

Will stood up and waved. "Over here."

I rose to my feet and stared at them as they approached, ready to greet them. I didn't know who was who, but when my eyes took in one of them everything stopped. Time seemed to halt, the universe coming to a standstill just so I could look at her more closely. Everything became silent. The distant conversations from other tables died away. The light tapping of forks against plates ceased altogether. Now it didn't feel like we were in a restaurant at all—but somewhere else entirely. I was on a new plane of existence. Every time my heart beat, it echoed in my ears like a war drum.

A distant hue burned around the edges of her silhouette. An invisible sun burned directly behind her, lighting her on fire and giving her the spotlight. She outshined everyone in the room— and everything.

Her brown hair reached past her shoulders and it had a red tint to it. Under the limited light of the restaurant, I could see the way it shined. Without touching it, I knew it was unnaturally soft. It framed her face in an elegant way, showing her prominent cheekbones.

Her eyes were stunning.

They were hazel but not just any hazel. They contained specks of various colors like yellow, orange, and even black. They were unusual, even strange. But they were hypnotically beautiful.

She wore a black dress that looked too loose on her. It didn't hug her waist the way it should, and it bunched around her shoulders because it didn't fit her skeletal frame correctly. But despite that, she still looked beautiful. This woman could wear a burlap sack and still look painfully gorgeous.

She was slender, barely containing an ounce of fat on her frame. I never cared for skinny girls, but I liked her. Her legs were long and toned, and her arms contained the same muscle definition.

She was perfect.

I was never nervous around anyone. It was impossible to intimidate me or shake my confidence. But now my mouth was drier than a desert, and I couldn't remember my name. I was even a little light-headed the closer she came. Anxiety burned in my chest because I didn't know what to do. What did I say? She put me on edge.

Her eyes locked to mine, and she didn't blink. She stared at me the same way I stared at her. Her thoughts were a mystery and impossible to decipher, but they were intriguing all the same. Her lips were full and kissable. Somehow, I think that was my favorite feature of hers.

I'd do anything to kiss her.

She slowly approached me, her hands gripping the black clutch in front of her waist. That intense stare still burned into my clothes and skin. When she was a foot away from me she stopped. She didn't speak or move her lips.

I didn't say anything either.

Words left me in that moment. There were so many things I wanted to say, but I had nothing to say at the exact same time. The background was still a blur. Everyone's faces were indistinguishable. The conversations died away. All I could see was she.

I'd never felt my body twist and tense like this. My arms burned from the constant contraction, and my lungs ached because they needed more air than I was allowing. My heart was the only thing that stayed calm. It was beating at a much slower pace than before.

I wanted to kiss her right then and there.

"Kyle." I wanted to say more, but my mouth was too dry. I extended my hand to shake hers.

She eyed it for a moment, full of hesitation. Then she looked back into my eyes before she slowly slid her hand into my grasp.

We didn't grip each other in a formal handshake. Actually, I just held her hand. My fingers wrapped around hers, and I felt her distant pulse. Her skin was soft and warm, and I felt my heart rate pick up the longer I touched her. I didn't let go because I didn't want to.

She eyed our hands again before she looked up at me. "Rose."

My heart stopped. Like I lost everything that mattered to me, my stomach burned in acid, and my lungs stopped breathing altogether. Panic swept over me in waves, followed by anxiety. It was a blow right to the chest, and it hurt long after the initial hit. "You aren't Florence…?"

"You aren't Will?"

"No." My jaw hurt just from giving that answer.

She slowly pulled her hand away until our fingers no longer touched. The second her hand was gone my body froze over. "It's nice to meet you..."

"Kyle." I already introduced myself, but I repeated my name anyway. All sense of logic went out the window the second we were in the same room.

"Kyle." She said my name slowly, enunciating every syllable.

Then we stood there and stared at each other, everything around us forgotten.

"Good job, Florence," Will said. "She's gorgeous."

"I know," Florence said. "So is the guy you brought for me."

I forgot about my date. The second Rose stepped into the room everything else seemed irrelevant.

Florence walked up to me, a flirtatious smile on her face. She had bright blue eyes and beautiful skin. "It's so nice to meet you." She extended her hand.

It was difficult for me to look away from Rose. It physically caused me pain to do so. "You too." My hand grabbed hers, and I gave her a firm handshake. I didn't feel the same heat as I did with Rose. If anything, it felt like we were having a job interview. Florence was pretty, and if I saw her first, I'd probably be attracted to her, but since I spotted Rose first I felt absolutely nothing.

Nothing.

Will walked up to Rose and extended his hand. "It's such a pleasure to meet you."

She eyed it closely before she took it. Unlike her handshake with me, she gripped him firmly before she dropped her hand. "You too." She automatically took a step back, putting space between them. Her eyes scanned the restaurant and looked at anything else but him. She seemed uneasy staring at him straight on.

"Shall we?" Florence walked to her chair and sat down.

I didn't pull it out like I normally would on a date. I was in a daze, confused and uneasy. I lowered myself in the chair and tried not to stare at Rose. She sat on the opposite side of the table next to Florence.

I'd have to stop myself from staring.

"So, you're a lawyer?" Florence leaned over the table with her elbows resting on the surface. Her enthusiasm was obvious.

"Yeah. I practice criminal law." My eyes darted to Rose to get a peek.

Her hair had been pulled over one shoulder, revealing beautiful skin that my lips ached to touch. Her eyes were downcast to her menu and she was silent, not engaging in conversation with Will.

"Wow," Florence said. "That's impressive."

I kept my eyes focused on her so they wouldn't get distracted. "Thanks. I love my job. What do you do?"

"I work in IT."

"Cool." It was impossible not to look at Rose. My eyes wanted to scream in protest when I wouldn't allow it. If I kept gawking at her, it would be rude to Florence. I didn't want to be an ass.

Will was smitten with Rose. He was just as obsessed with her as I was. His wide eyes never relaxed because he was surprised his blind date turned out to be a supermodel. "What do you do, Rose?"

"I'm an architect," she said quietly.

"Seriously?" I blurted it out before I could stop myself. "That's so cool." I'd never known an architect before. They were the people who built our skyscrapers and our landmarks. The creativity as well as the mathematics required for the job was impressive.

She looked at me for a split second. "Thanks. I like it."

I caught myself gawking all over again so I turned back to Florence.

"That is cool," Will said. "Have you designed any buildings?"

"A few," she said. "You know the Lincoln Building?"

"Yeah," Will answered.

"That was me," she said quietly.

"Awesome," he said. "I've never known an architect before."

"Well, now you do." She gave him a smile before she looked down at her menu again.

"I'm an engineer," Will said. "So, our jobs are kind of similar."

"What kind of engineer are you?" Rose asked.

"Mechanical."

"Cool." She took a long drink of her water, downing nearly the entire glass. Her mouth was just as parched as mine. She didn't just seem nervous but also uncomfortable.

I was looking at her again so I forced myself to stop. She wasn't my date, and I needed to back off. I turned back to Florence and tried to think of something to say. "My mother is in

31

Florence right now. Are you named after the city?"

"She is?" she asked. "Actually, I think my parents just liked the name."

I nodded. "Cool." Despite the way she kept smiling at me, I didn't feel any chemistry at all. Every time I tried to stay focused, I thought of another question I wanted to ask Rose.

"Are you from New York?" Will asked.

"Yes," Rose answered. "Born and raised." She held the menu like it was a shield, keeping him back. "What about you?"

"Yeah," Will answered. "I can't see myself living anywhere else."

Rose stared at the menu.

When I looked back at Florence she was staring at me hard. "What do you do for fun?" Our conversation was strenuous and choppy. It didn't flow well like it should. If anything, we were forcing it.

"I like jogging. I jog through the park every morning."

"Cool." I couldn't think of a better response so I kept using the same one over and over.

"You must work out a lot."

32

"Uh, I guess." It wasn't a question so I wasn't sure what to say. "Do you like sports?"

She shrugged. "Sorta. I don't follow anything religiously."

Will nudged me in the side. "This guy is in love with Stephen Curry. I think he's a joke."

"He's a great player," Rose said, her eyes still on the menu.

My head snapped in her direction, hoping she would look at me. "That's what I keep saying."

She took another drink of her water even though there were only a few drops left. Clearly flustered, she turned back to her menu and tried to withdraw as much as possible.

"So, you like sports?" Will asked. "Anything besides basketball?"

"I like hockey." She set her menu down then abruptly stood up. "Excuse me." She moved through the sea of tables and headed to the bathroom.

When she was gone, a cloud of tension fell over the table.

My eyes followed her movements through the entire restaurant until she disappeared into the bathroom. She had wide hips, the kind that gave her a full figure. When she carried herself, her back was perfectly straight. She possessed an aura of elegance.

Will turned to Florence when she was gone. "Damn, she's hot."

My hand immediately formed a fist, and I wanted to punch him hard in the jaw.

"Where did you find her?" Will asked.

"We've been friends since college," Florence answered.

"You need to set me up on blind dates more often," he said. "You know all the sexy ones."

Now my knuckles were turning white.

Will glanced at the bathroom before he turned back to her. "She's pretty quiet. Is she just shy?"

Florence broke eye contact and looked at the table. Her fingers met and she fidgeted in place. "Yeah...she's just shy."

Even though I just met her, I knew she was lying. There was more to this story, but I doubted I'd get to the bottom of it.

"She doesn't date much," Florence said. "I had to give her a push to come out tonight."

I wondered why she didn't date much. Did she recently get out of a relationship?

"Okay," Will said. "I'll go easy on her."

My eyes kept moving to the bathroom, waiting for her to come out.

Florence turned her gaze on me, her natural smile coming through. "Want to share a bottle of wine?"

"Sure." I wasn't a big wine person. I preferred beer most of the time.

"White or red?"

It didn't matter. "Your choice."

She grabbed the wine list and looked through it, her eyes downcast. Her leg moved under the table until it brushed against mine. She rubbed it seductively, making it clear she didn't touch me by mistake.

Rose stepped out of the bathroom and headed back to the table, and my eyes were on her the entire way. I watched the way her hips shook as she moved, and I noticed the way she stared at the ground as she walked. She lacked confidence of any kind, but she still projected strength.

My date was really into me, judging the way she continued to rub my leg under the table. Her eyes were on me nearly the entire time, staring at my face and my broad shoulders.

But all I noticed was Rose.

***

Saturday

We stood outside the restaurant together, the cars passing by on the street. It was a warm summer's night and the breeze that drifted on the wind gave us some respite from the humidity.

My eyes moved to Rose's legs more than once.

"Thank you for dinner." Florence moved into my chest, taking up more space than I was prepared to give.

"You're welcome." I forced myself to stare into her face. "Thank you for spending the evening with me."

"The pleasure was all mine. Maybe we can do it again sometime."

Against my will, my eyes moved to Rose.

"Can I walk you home?" Will moved his arm around her waist.

Rose turned slightly, avoiding the affection without making it seem obvious. "That's sweet, but I can make it on my own."

"Can I call you a taxi?" Will asked.

"No, I'll just get an Uber or something." She tucked her hair behind her ear and took another step back.

"I'd really love to go out again," Will said. "There's this new Mediterranean place I've been wanting to try."

Her lips pressed tightly together, showing her distress. Her fingers were latched around her clutch tightly, squeezing it so tightly her knuckles were turning white. "Thank you for the offer, but I'm pretty busy…"

"Oh…" Will couldn't hide his disappointment. He rubbed the back of his neck then looked at the ground. "Uh, okay."

Florence watched their interaction just the way I did. "Give us a moment." She grabbed Rose by the arm and dragged her a few feet away. Her voice was low enough so neither one of us could hear what they were saying.

"I don't get it," Will said. "I was nothing but nice to her."

"I'm sure it's nothing personal." Will was a good friend, but he didn't deserve her. She needed to be with someone better—someone like me.

The girls came back, and Rose had the same look of unease on her face that she'd been wearing all night.

Florence finally released her arm. "Rose would love to go out with you again."

"I don't need you to talk for me," Rose snapped.

Florence brushed off the outburst. "She's free tomorrow night."

"Awesome," Will said. "How about I pick you up at seven?"

"I'll just meet you there." She pulled out her phone from her clutch and looked at the time. "Well, I really should get going. Thank you for dinner, Will."

"Anytime."

Rose turned to me to say goodbye. But instead of saying anything she just stared at me. Of everyone in that group, I was the only person she made eye contact with. Even though we hadn't had a real conversation, there was some connection there. "Good night, Kyle."

CHAPTER FIVE

Kyle

All I could think about was Rose.

The way her hair fell around her face excited me in ways I couldn't explain with words. The attraction was carnal and innate, like my body was unable to control its reaction to her features. I craved her endlessly, wanting her in so many ways.

When her eyes looked into mine, there was more than just a look. Entire conversations happened in nanoseconds. My body felt hot and cold at the same time. Instantly, I would shiver then melt.

She was shorter than the women I usually dated, almost a foot shorter. Even in heels she was petite. But I loved her form and her size. She was perfect enough to sleep right on my chest.

Saturday

Throughout the whole night, I only said a few words to her. There wasn't even enough exchange to make a general opinion about her. I really didn't know her and I certainly didn't understand her.

But I was obsessed.

Florence was a nice woman and she was pretty. She was forward and confident, something I found innately attractive. If Rose hadn't been there at all, Florence and I probably would have hit it off.

But Rose was there.

Florence couldn't keep my attention for more than a few seconds at any given point in time. I didn't think about kissing her or feeling her body with my bare hands. If I invited her to my place at the end of the night, she probably would have come along.

But I didn't want that.

I was sitting in my office when Will called me.

"Hey, what's up?" I put my feet on the desk and looked out the floor-to-ceiling windows.

"How'd it go with Florence?"

"What do you mean? You were there."

"Did you take her back to your place?"

"No." I couldn't sleep with someone while thinking of someone else.

"Really? It seemed like she was into you."

"Well, I wasn't into her." Why did Will have to get Rose? Why did he have to get the one woman I was unbelievably attracted to? I'd never stopped in my tracks because of a woman in my life. She floored me with just her presence. But then Will got her.

"Really?" he asked. "Florence is pretty cute."

"Then why don't you go out with her?" I was letting my jealousy get the best of me, but I couldn't help it.

"She's my friend. It would be weird."

I suspected Rose didn't even like him. It sure didn't seem like it.

"That's too bad," he said. "Rose said she wanted to go on another double date."

That had my attention. "Yeah?"

"I wanted it just to be her and me, but she insisted on the two of you coming along."

It sounded like she didn't want to be alone with Will. Or she wanted to see me again.

"But if you don't like Florence, we'll just have to make do without."

"Whoa, hold on." I wasn't going to pass up an excuse to see Rose. I was already stuck with Florence and I couldn't just ditch her for her friend, but I couldn't help myself. Just being in her presence gave me a high I couldn't describe. "Florence and I will be there."

"I thought you said you didn't like her?"

"I'll give her another chance."

"Are you sure?" he asked.

"Absolutely." Even if I didn't get to talk to Rose directly I wanted to be in her presence. To feel that rush, that high, was something I longed for. Maybe our first interaction was purely physical infatuation. Maybe if I saw her again it would disappear.

***

I got there nearly thirty minutes early just in case Rose showed up before the others. I wanted an opportunity to speak to her without the other two around. When the four of us were at the dinner table I was forced to focus on Florence. But if the situation was different, I could focus on something else.

To my luck, Rose arrived fifteen minutes early. She wore denim shorts with a pink top. Her hair was pulled back in a high ponytail, revealing all the beautiful curves of her face. Her eyes stood out the most, hypnotizing and alluring.

She spotted me standing outside, and she halted in her tracks. She watched me for a few seconds before she approached me, her eyes glued to my face. A loose strand of hair fell from her ponytail and trailed down the side of her cheek.

My hands were in my pockets, giving the impression that I was calm and collected. After our first encounter I suspected the second one to be more subdued. My heart would beat calmly and my body would remain relaxed.

But that's not what happened.

Just like last time my heart ached in pain. My muscles tensed uncomfortably and my breathing became irregular. My physiological response to her was unusual, something I've never experienced before. I was both nervous and eager at the same time.

Rose gripped her clutch with one hand, the same one she had last time we went out together. Instead of looking down at the ground or avoiding my look she stared at me straight on.

"Hi." It took more energy than normal to get that word out. I was even a little breathless.

"Hey." She took a deep breath once she finished.

Now I didn't know what else to do. It wasn't like me to be tongue-tied. Actually, I couldn't shut up most of the time. This woman left me speechless. "How are you?"

"Good. You?"

"Great. Except the fact I'm missing the Warrior game right now."

For the first time, she smiled. "I know. I was bummed too."

"I'm recording it so don't tell me the score."

"I'm recording it too. I wanted to see every play and every shot."

Now that we were in a conversation my body relaxed slightly. "What else do you like?"

"Hockey."

"Pretty violent sport."

She shrugged. "I guess I like the fact they don't have as many rules. It can be ruthless and terrifying, but that's what makes it so unique."

"I know what you mean."

"Do you like anything else?"

"Everything. Mainly baseball and football."

She shook her head. "I don't care too much for those."

I kept my hands in my pockets so I wouldn't fidget in place. She made me nervous, but I didn't want her to know what kind of effect she had on me. "Did you work today?"

"Yeah."

"Where do you work?"

"I'm a freelancer," she answered. "I work whenever I'm hired. I have a small office here in Manhattan, but I get outsourced to do other jobs in different places."

"Very cool. So, you're your own boss."

"Essentially."

She and I were the same in that regard. "Do you like it?"

"I love it," she said. "There's nothing like making someone's dream home. Or making a design that will survive hundreds of years after I'm gone. It's an amazing feeling."

"I can imagine."

She crossed her arms over her chest, her clutch held tightly against her side. It was the first time she turned away, her eyes glued to the road.

"You like Will?" I suspected I already knew the answer, but I asked anyway.

"He's nice…"

My body wanted to close the gap between us and press my mouth to hers. My body was obsessed with hers to the point of insanity. And I didn't just want her physically. I wanted to know everything underneath.

"You like Florence?"

I shrugged. "She's nice…"

She nodded and still refused to meet my gaze.

"Dating isn't really your thing?" I hated myself for asking a personal question I had no right asking. It just came out all on its own. I would never say something like that to any other stranger. For whatever reason, I thought it was okay to say it to her.

"No. Not really." She looked at me again, her eyes bright and beautiful.

"Then why are you doing it?"

She shrugged. "It'll make Florence happy. I have to try—for her."

I wanted to know more. Actually, I want to know everything. "Did you just get out of a relationship?"

Before she could answer, she spotted Florence and Will over my shoulder. "They're here."

I still wanted that answer.

"Hey." Florence moved into my chest and hugged me. Before I knew what was going on she kissed me on the lips. "I'm so excited to see you."

She caught me off guard and gave me the kind of affection I didn't even want, but the damage was already done. "Hey." I took a step back before she kissed me again. "Hungry?"

"Very."

Will was immediately at her side. "I've been looking forward to this all week."

"Me too," Rose said quietly.

We went inside and took our seats near the window. Just like last time, it was awkward. Rose tried to hide behind her menu and Florence was feeling me up under the table. If her hand could reach all the way across, she'd probably be giving me a hand job right then and there.

***

By the end of the night, Florence was all over me. "You should come to my place. I have a nice view of the park."

"Uh, maybe." I didn't want to sleep with her, not when I was interested in Rose.

"Or maybe we can go to yours..." Her leg had practically rubbed my jeans off.

I knew I got myself into a deep hole. I'd led her on and now she wanted me—naked. It was stupid for me to agree to this date just to see Rose. I suspected this would blow up in my face very soon.

Will and I split the bill then left our table, the girls by our sides. Florence hooked her arm through mine and pressed her body against me. She whispered something in my ear. "You're mine tonight."

Shit.

We walked outside then congregated off to the side away from the foot traffic. Rose still kept to herself, not showing Will any affection. She clung to her clutch like it was a lifeboat.

"Let's head to my place." Florence had become even more forward after a few drinks. I was attracted to confident women who knew exactly what they wanted, but it was a turn off when they were drunk—and bossy.

"Can I walk you home?" Will asked the same question as last time, and he would get the same answer.

"It's okay." Rose extended her hand to shake his. "I had a great time."

He eyed her hand in disappointment. He hadn't touched her once, besides her hand. "Me too..." I shook it with a grimace.

"Well, good night." Rose walked away without saying goodbye to me. She fled the scene like she couldn't get away fast enough. All she wanted was to please her friend, and now that she was done she was on her way.

Florence didn't seem to notice because of all of her attention was on me. "Come on. Let's go." She yanked my arm aggressively.

Now I was getting tired of being dragged around like a dog. "Enough of that." I pulled out of her grasp and put my hands in my pockets. "Where is your apartment?"

She smiled because she thought she was getting her way. "This way."

***

I walked her to her door because she wouldn't have made it there on her own.

She dropped her keys a few times before she got the door opened. "The highlight of the night..." She walked inside and immediately kicked her heels off.

I stayed on the other side of the door. "Good night, Florence."

"What?" Her eyes were squinted in her drunken stupor, and her body was tense in hostility.

"Florence, this isn't going to work out. But I wanted to walk you home to make sure you got here safely."

"You aren't coming inside?"

I shook my head.

"Why the hell not?" She put both hands on her hips, glaring at me violently.

"It's not you," I said calmly. "You're a very attractive woman—"

"Obviously."

But not very humble. "But I'm just feeling it. I wish you the best of luck."

"Are you gay or something?" she snapped.

I let the insult wash over me. She was drunk and not running at full capacity. "Definitely not." I turned away and headed down the hall. "Good night, Florence."

"Good night, asshole."

CHAPTER SIX

Kyle

"Carol, could you come in here for a moment?" I just finished doing a search of every architect company in the city but didn't find any leads, not even with her name affiliated with it. Who knew so many architect companies existed at all.

Carol walked inside with her notepad and pen at the ready. "Yes, Kyle?"

"I need help with something."

"Of course. What can I do for you?" She took a seat and crossed her legs.

"I need help finding a girl."

"A girl...?"

I understood how strange my request sounded. I could ask Will for her number, but that would probably piss him off. And I certainly couldn't go to Florence with my questions. After the way our relationship ended, she wouldn't help me with a damn thing. "I met her a week ago. She runs an architect company and her name is Rose. I tried tracking her down myself but with no luck. Maybe you'll have better success."

"Do you have any other information?"

"No."

"Is this company in Manhattan?"

"Yes. That I do know."

She left the chair and closed her notepad. "I'll do my best. But I'm not a PI so don't expect anything."

"Whatever you can manage is appreciated."

***

Mark walked into the office, looking lower than I've ever seen him. He fell into the chair and leaned forward, gripping his skull in anguish. While he was silent for the time being, he was about to explode.

I knew he lost his case.

"Mark, you can't win them all." I took the seat beside him and tried to console him as much as possible.

"But I should have won this one."

I patted him on the back. "You did the best you could, man. There was nothing else you could have done."

"Tell that to her parents. Tell that to her sister." He refused to meet my gaze, his cheeks turning red with rage. "The judge threw out that evidence when she shouldn't have. It was totally unfair. What the hell is wrong with our legal system?"

What the hell was wrong with our world, actually? "Mark, you have to let it go."

"I don't think I can..."

"It's impossible to win every case. Sometimes the defendant has more ammo in his arsenal. Sometimes you get a bad judge. Sometimes the jury is the one at fault. Cut yourself some slack."

He left the chair, getting away from my affection. "She was raped and murdered." He rested his fist against his lips, his eyes closed from the rage. "And the fucker got away. You expect me to cut myself some slack?" He turned to me, his eyes red and bloodshot. "What if that were your sister? Your girlfriend?"

I'd already been through that once—and it was the worst experience of my life. "You can't win them all." I felt like a parrot repeating myself, but it was the only thing that came to mind. It was easy to lose sleep over our cases. It was easy to lose ourselves too. But we had to stay sane, to remember there was only so much we could do in any given situation. "Maybe you should take the rest of the week off—with pay."

"That's not going to solve my problem."

I slowly approached him, not wanting to push him even further. "Take some time to clear your head. Go to the beach. Take a trip. Just take some time for yourself. This business can be daunting. It's best to pace ourselves."

He stared at the ground, his eyes lifeless.

I knew exactly how he felt, but I could never tell him that. Some people in the office knew what happened all those years ago but a lot of them didn't. I liked to keep my private life to myself as possible. Otherwise old wounds would fester and become infected all over again.

He finally nodded. "I think I should."

I clapped him on the shoulder again. "Great. I think that will be best."

***

A few days later I got a lead.

"Kyle, I have a name and an address." Carol placed the note on my desk. "I'm pretty sure this is the girl you're looking for. It's just a few blocks away."

I snatched it from the surface.

INDIGO DESIGNS.

"You're sure?"

"From what the leasing information I pulled up, it said a woman named Rose was the tenant. That was the best I could do."

I shoved the note into my pocket, feeling my lips automatically form a smile. "Thank you."

***

Her office was a tiny little place above a Chinese food restaurant. It had to be four hundred square feet at the most. And with a location like that, I suspected she didn't pick up a lot of foot traffic.

So why have an office at all?

I made it to the second floor then walked past the windows. They were tinted so I couldn't see anything inside. Just before I walked inside, I stopped because I panicked. Now that I was here I didn't know what to say. Did I just ask her out? Did I act like I needed work? What should I do?

If she was looking at me through the window, I must look strange.

I straightened my shoulders and walked inside with confidence. Rose was shy and withdrawn, but every woman responded to a man who knew what he wanted. The bell rang overhead the moment I walked inside, and then I came face-to-face with her.

She was sitting at her small desk with an iPad on the surface. Judging the surprise on her face she didn't get very many customers. I was probably the only person to walk inside that day—or maybe even that week.

Rose's eyes narrowed slightly when she recognized me. She didn't move from her desk, remaining absolutely still. Even her breathing didn't change.

I stepped further inside and felt the nerves get to me. She was staring at me intently, unsure why I was there and what I wanted. That confidence I felt a moment ago was dissipating. Like she was the sun, my confidence evaporated from my skin. "Hi. I hope this isn't a bad time."

"No. I'm just surprised to see you."

I was surprised too. "I was in the neighborhood and thought I would stop by."

"How did you know I worked here?"

"You told me."

"No, I didn't." Her clipped tone suddenly turned hostile.

Maybe this was a bad idea. "Well, I looked it up online. It was pretty easy to find."

That same threat was still on her face.

Did I just screw this up? "I'm sorry if I've done something to offend you. I didn't see the harm in coming here. If you want me to leave, I'll go." She never behaved this way in our previous interactions, but now she was a wild animal cornered against the wall. Frightened and uncomfortable, she was about to lash out. I took a step back toward the door so she knew I meant it.

"No, it's okay." She shook her head like she realized her mistake. She was being rude when I'd done nothing to deserve it. "What can I help you with?"

"Like I said, I was in the neighborhood and thought I'd stop by."

That wasn't the answer she was hoping for. "Well, it was nice to see you, but I should be getting back to work." She grabbed her stylist and returned to her iPad like the conversation was over.

Why did I always like the unattainable women? First, it was Francesca and now Rose.

I put my hands in my pocket and approached her desk. It was made of white wood with pastel blue organizers on top. The entire room was decorated in bright colors, yellow, pink, and white.

A smart guy would give up because he knew this was pointless. But I was definitely not smart. In fact, I was as dumb as they come. "I just inherited a large piece of property in the Hamptons and now I need someone to design a home for me. If you're interested, I'd love to talk about it." Most of that was true. When my father passed, he had a lot of wealth that wasn't placed within a trust. It went to his lawyers, who kicked it around until it was finally cleared to fall in my hands. It took nearly five years to finally get it.

"You inherited property?" she asked. "I'm sorry..." She forgot about her iPad and looked up at me, the sincerity shining in her eyes.

"Thanks. My father passed away seven years ago. It's taken a very long time for some of his wealth to finally fall into my hands."

She nodded in understanding, like she'd been through the same thing. "Take a seat."

I sat in the chair facing her desk and realized how close we were to one another. In fact, it was the closest we'd ever been.

And we were alone.

I didn't have any ideas for the property I attained. In fact, I was going to let it sit there for a long time before I figured out what to do with it. I could sell it for a good price as it was. But now I used it as an excuse to talk with Rose.

"Is there something specific you had in mind?"

Since I had to come up with ideas on the spot, no. "Not really. It's going to be my dream home, the place where I retire, and I want an expert to help me along."

"I've worked on a lot of homes so you'll be in safe hands." When she spoke of her profession, she was surprisingly calm. It made her feel safe because it was her element. But once she was pulled out of that she was a different person.

Today she did her hair differently than the other times I'd seen it. It was curled in spirals, and it was pulled over one shoulder. Make up was on her face, more than it was the other night. Her eyelashes were thick and long, and the eyeliner under her eyes made them stand out. The foundation on her skin blended perfectly into her face. With makeup, she was gorgeous. Without it, she was still gorgeous.

She pulled out a notebook and a pencil. "Do you have any pictures?"

"Of what?" The house that I hadn't even begun to build?

"Of the land. I need to know where it is, how big it is, and what's around it."

I shook my head in response. "Sorry, I don't."

"That's okay," she said. "Do you have any at home?"

"Actually, no." I didn't see the point in taking a picture of the bare land, especially since I never planned on doing anything with it.

"Well, I need that information before I start."

I didn't realize how genius this idea was until that moment. "Let's drive out and take a look at it. You can see it first hand and we can take some pictures." Now I'd be able to spend the whole day with her—maybe even the night.

She pressed the end of the pencil to her bottom lip while she stared at the blank paper. The expression was thoughtful—and distinctly cute. "How far is the drive?"

"About three hours." It was actually two, but she didn't need to know that.

"Hmm..."

"It's far for a day trip," I said. "But I have another beach house just a few miles from the property. We can crash there then come back." With a little alone time, I could charm her into a date.

"You have another beach house?" she asked incredulously.

"Yeah. But I bought that one." I didn't want her to think I was a spoiled jerk that got everything from my parents.

"It's always interesting to see how the other side lives..."

"So, what do you say? We can take a trip out there tomorrow, spend the night, and then head back."

Her eyes immediately broke contact and she sat back against her chair, putting invisible space between us. "I'll stay at a hotel."

"A hotel?" I asked. "All the resorts there are expensive." Like, crazy expensive. I could barely afford to vacation there.

"Then I'll stay at a motel."

Had she never been to the Hamptons? "There's no such thing as a motel there. Really, it's fine. We can just crash at my place. There's lots of bedrooms and space."

"No." She looked down again and grew flustered. Her breathing became irregular and her skin had a distinct red tint to it. "We'll drive separately and I'll come back when the work is finished."

That was even worse.

Did she not trust me? Did she think I was a weirdo? How did I fix this mess I just got into? "How about this? You can stay at my beach place and I'll crash with my mom. She lives right down the road."

The fear slowly drained from her face. "I don't want to impose on you."

"You wouldn't be imposing," I said. "I'm never there anyway and my mom loves any excuse to see me. I could just walk into her house and she'd be thrilled." That was the honest truth. After my sister died, she clung to me even harder, afraid I might slip away too.

"If you're sure that's okay, we can do that."

Perfect. Now I could spend the whole day with her—and the one after that. "It's more than okay."

CHAPTER SEVEN

Rose

Florence walked inside, and judging the way the skies darkened around her as she moved, she wasn't happy. "You won't believe what that asshole did."

"What asshole?" I had my suitcase sitting by the door with all my stuff packed inside. Getting a physical view of the place was exactly what I needed before I began building the model. It was the best inspiration I could ever receive.

"Kyle."

In his defense, she thought everyone was an asshole. "What did he do?"

"When we went out last weekend he walked me to my door then dumped me." She flipped her hair over her shoulder in an irritated way. "He didn't even give me an explanation. He just said we were over."

Saturday

At least he didn't sleep with her and never call her again like most guys. Florence always assumed every guy was out to get her, but she never assumed any responsibility when things went wrong. "You only went out twice. Maybe he just didn't feel anything."

"Whatever. He's still an ass."

I didn't bother correcting her because she was too stubborn. We would just get into a fight that would blow up in my face. It was better just to let the conversation die. "Sorry, it didn't work out. I know you liked him."

"God, he was hot." She sighed in longing. "He's the most beautiful man I've ever seen in my life."

I couldn't deny he was easy on the eyes. It was the first thought that crossed my mind when I looked at him. "There are other fish in the sea, Florence."

"I guess." Now that her tantrum was over she looked at my suitcase by the door. "Where are you going?"

I had to tell her the truth—even if she got upset. "Kyle hired me to build his beach house in the Hamptons. We're going to take a look at it tomorrow."

"Hold on." She held up her hand, her attitude firing up again. "He has a beach house?"

I shrugged. "Two, apparently."

"Ugh." She stomped her foot and screamed. "Now I really hate him. He's a young, rich lawyer. Will told me he owns his own practice—and he's thirty. Can you believe that?"

"Some people are very driven."

"And he's hot as hell. Damn, why didn't it work out with us?"

Florence cared too much about social status and looks. She only went after doctors and lawyers, attracted to their wealth as well as their intelligence. I didn't judge her for it, but it wasn't my style. "Florence, you'll find the right guy someday." When she started looking for the right guy.

"So, you didn't like Will?" She came to the couch and sat beside me. Now she became calm and adopted her inside voice.

"He was nice…" He was smart and polite, but I didn't see it going anywhere. But then again, I didn't see it going anywhere with anyone. If Florence didn't force me to go on these random dates, I'd stick to my asexual lifestyle.

"Come on, there's nothing wrong with him. Give him a chance."

"Florence, I appreciate what you're trying to do, but it's not working. When I'm ready, it'll happen. But for right now, I need more time." Honestly, I didn't see myself being with another man as long as I lived—and preferred it that way.

She gave me that look she always gave me—one of disappointment. "I'm not trying to be insensitive, but you need to move on with your life."

Unless she'd been through what I'd been through, she had no right to push me. "I will—in time. Can we stop doing these blind dates now?"

"I guess so. Since they're a waste of time anyway..."

"I need to get back to packing." I just wanted an excuse for her to leave. These conversations always left me dead inside.

"How long will you be gone?"

"A few days."

"Where are you staying?"

"At Kyle's place."

"Whoa, what?" Her temper flared up out of nowhere.

"I'm staying at his beach house while he stays with his mom." Like I'd ever stay in the same house with a guy I barely knew. I'd drive home before I had to resort to that.

Her anger deflated like a balloon. "You had me worried for a second."

"You know me better than that, Florence."

***

Kyle pulled up in a sleek sports car. It was charcoal gray with a roaring engine to boot. I didn't know much about cars, and I didn't have a clue what kind this one was.

But it was nice.

He got out of the car wearing aviator sunglasses. A grin stretched his lips as he walked around the back to meet me on the sidewalk. "Ready?"

"Yeah. I just hope my suitcase will fit." I could barely carry it down to the sidewalk because it was so heavy. It was eighty inches long so I wasn't sure if it would fit in the trunk.

"It will." He popped the trunk then picked up the suitcase like it weighed nothing. "I've put bodies back here before."

My blood ran cold.

He shoved the suitcase inside then closed the back. "Kidding, sweetheart."

"Oh…" I tried to laugh it off like I knew it was a joke.

He opened the passenger door for me. "Don't worry, I'm not a criminal. And I'm a great driver. You're in safe hands." He pulled up his sunglasses and rested them on his head so I could see his face. His blue eyes were bright and vibrant, the pretty kind girls always loved.

"Good to know." I ducked then got into the car. Once I was inside, I felt the cold leather under my skin. The engine was loud, even from inside. The dashboard was sleek and pristine. It even smelled new.

Kyle got into the driver's seat and fastened his seat belt. "You have everything?"

"Yeah."

"Okay." He pulled into traffic and made his way out of the city.

***

Once we left the bridge, we drove along the coastline. He rolled down his window and let the fresh air into the car. Driving his fancy car gave him obvious satisfaction.

Boys with their toys.

"Thanks for coming along."

"No problem." Going to the beach wasn't the worst way to spend my day. It was nice to be outside rather than cooped up in my office, making blueprints for the engineers. Now I could breathe the fresh air.

"How long have you been running your office?"

"A few years," I answered. "I know it's small, but if I work from home, I won't work at all."

He chuckled. "Yeah, I get that."

I already knew a lot about him from Florence. She gushed about him left and right—before he dumped her. "So, you run a law firm?"

"Yeah, I'm the senior partner."

It was a big accomplishment for a thirty-year-old. "That's impressive."

"It's not as impressive as it sounds. My dad opened it thirty years ago. When he passed away, I took over."

"Oh...I'm sorry." Running his father's legacy must make him happy and sad at the same time.

"I always knew I would take it over someday, but I didn't expect to do that so soon." He drove with one hand on the wheel while the other rested on the gearshift. The coastline was in the background, and Kyle spent just as much time looking at me as he did looking at the road. "It's an honor to work for his firm because we have a lot of great lawyers. I love being a part of it."

"Do you like being a lawyer?" It seemed more complicated than regular jobs. When they left the courtroom, did they really clock out? Or did they go home and think about everything that happened that day? Did they think about the clients they let down?

"There's nothing else I'd rather do. But there are days when I hate it—like any other job."

I didn't hate my job at all. In fact, I adored it. To me, it was fun.

"It can be stressful taking on a case. And when you lose a case you really care about, it haunts you."

"I can imagine."

"I work with criminal cases a lot, like homicide, child abuse, sexual assault, rape, stuff like that...it can be heartbreaking sometimes."

I quickly looked away and stared out the passenger window, not wanting him to catch a glimpse of my face. There was a knot in my throat so I swallowed it, but it was painful all the way down.

"I haven't lost a case myself, but I know people who have. It really eats them away." The radio was on in the background so he turned it off altogether. "Are you okay?"

"I'm fine. Just looking at the scenery."

"Enough about me," he said. "When did you know you wanted to be an architect?"

I remembered the exact moment. "Did you play with Legos as a kid?"

"Psh. I still play with Legos." The same beautiful grin was on his face, making him look even more handsome.

"Well, I used to play with those a lot as a child. I would build towers, castles, and buildings...I knew then that I wanted to do it forever."

"That's cute."

I turned back to him, my eyebrow raised.

"I'm picturing you as a little girl sitting on the floor playing with Legos...I'm sure it was cute."

I smiled before I looked away.

He drummed his fingers gently on the wheel as he cruised down the highway. There were no other cars in sight, and the road seemed to be paved just for us. "So...are you not seeing Will anymore?"

I suspected this would come up eventually. "I wasn't planning on it." They were friends, so hopefully Kyle would pass on the message if Will wanted to ask me out again.

"On our second date, you mentioned you didn't like the dating scene…any particular reason why?"

I didn't want to be interrogated about it, but I couldn't hold it against him for asking. After all, I did divulge that information to begin with. "I prefer to be alone." I wasn't going to tell him the truth. It was one of those secrets you took to the grave.

His tone darkened, becoming serious. "No one likes to be alone…"

"Well, I do." Being alone was better than trying to move on with my life. It was just too painful. The times I tried, it just blew up in my face. Remaining detached and isolated was my only solution—and it worked for me.

Kyle didn't press me further on the topic. Somehow, he understood the conversation was no longer welcome. "I had a really painful break up about a year ago. It wasn't pretty."

I turned his way, intrigued.

"We were dating for a few months then she went back to her ex. Then a few months later, we started dating again. This time, I thought it was the end of the story. I thought we were going to be together forever. Just before I proposed, she left me again...for her ex." He had the strength to chuckle. "Joke's on me, right?"

"I'm sorry that happened to you."

"It's okay," he said. "I was devastated in the beginning but with every passing month, it got easier. And then six months later, I was over it. She's married and pregnant, and I'm happy for her."

"You're a good man." Most people would be bitter about it forever.

"And you know what they say about the good guys, right? They finish last."

***

"I know it's not much to look at, but this is it." He walked across the sand in his jeans and t-shirt. The wind had picked up slightly and ran through his hair. His Vans were getting covered in sand, but he didn't seem to mind. "Beach house number two will go right here."

It was a nice piece of land. The great thing about it was the fact it was isolated. There were no other homes around. Privacy was extremely valuable when it came to private homes. "Where is your property line?"

Kyle pointed in the distance. "Way out there..." Then he turned around and pointed in the other direction. "Way out there..."

So he owned a mile of the beach. His family must be even wealthier than I imagined.

"So, we have plenty of room."

"So, you don't want a beach house. You're looking for a mansion."

"Uh, not really," he said. "I want something big enough for a family of four."

"Why four?"

"My wife and two kids. They'll be living with me. Well...at least I hope they will." He chuckled while he watched me, seeing every expression I made. "Maybe a pool and a deck. But nothing too fancy."

I walked up and down the sand and tried to picture what I might design for him. He seemed like a man with simple tastes and pleasures. He would be easy to please unlike some of the diva clients I had.

When I moved across the sand, he watched me the entire time, keeping his gaze on me no matter where I went. I pulled out my notebook and made a few notes, taking down measurements and ground structure. It took me nearly thirty minutes to complete, wanting to gather as much information as possible while I was there. When I was finished, the sun was beginning to set.

"Pooped out?" Kyle asked.

"Something like that." I tucked my pen between the pages and closed the notebook. "I have a few ideas you might like."

"Perfect."

***

He pulled into the gate of his beach house and parked in the roundabout in front of the house. It was the average size of a home but beautiful in its design. It had a distinct beach feel to it, something I noticed in his personality as well.

"Home sweet home." Kyle grabbed my suitcase then walked into the house. "I hope you like it."

Like it was possible for me to dislike it. "It's beautiful."

He set the suitcase near the door then turned on all the lights. "The housecleaners come every two weeks even if I don't make a visit. So you don't have to worry about my cooties." He wiggled his eyebrows at me before he headed into the kitchen.

"What a relief." His furniture was white and gray, matching the color of the sand outside. The hardwood floors were dark, and the fireplace in the corner seemed perfect to combat the nighttime chill.

"What do you want for dinner?"

He was staying for dinner? I walked into the kitchen and saw him standing at the fridge.

"I had the housecleaners take care of the grocery shopping. We've got the basic necessities along with a few other things. How about steak kabobs? I'm pretty good on the grill."

I didn't want to kick him out of his own home, but I didn't expect to spend any alone time with him. "Uh, sure." We'd been alone together all day and everything was fine. I could handle this.

"Great." He pulled everything out and began to prep. He cleaned the vegetables then slid them onto the skewers along with chunks of meat.

"Do you need any help?"

"Nope. You're my guest." He grabbed a bottle of wine from the fridge. "Is white okay?"

"Sure."

He poured two glasses then carried the kabobs outside where the grill sat. It was located on the deck where the rest of the patio was.

I followed him outside and noticed how bright the ocean looked. The sun was sitting on the opposite side of the house, and it was bringing life to the waves. They crashed in the distance, sounding musical on my ears. "I'm surprised you don't live here and commute to work."

"Commuting is such a bitch." He got the grill going and laid the kabobs on the racks. "I tried it a few years ago and it just didn't work. Besides, I love living in the city. It's easy to get Chinese food at two in the morning."

"Do you eat Chinese food at two in the morning often?" I sat in the chair with the glass of wine in my hand.

"Sometimes," he said. "Not often." He turned the kabobs over and watched them cook. Then he closed the lid to keep the heat contained. With one hand resting on the handle of the grill, he watched me.

Whenever he looked at me that way, I grew uncomfortable. The stare wasn't hostile, but it still set me on edge. I could feel something develop deep inside my stomach. It gravitated toward the rest of my body, making me feel scorching hot and freezing cold at the same time. The look he gave me was unlike any other I'd received before. A part of me liked it—but that's what scared me the most.

Kyle opened the grill again and turned the kabobs. "How's Florence?"

"Uh...she's good." After everything she said about him, she was anything but good.

"Really?" he asked. "I was wondering if she still hated me."

I guess she told him to his face. "She's not your biggest fan."

He shrugged. "I was honest with her. I didn't see it going anywhere."

Florence was a good friend of mine, but I knew she had some emotional issues. She was too clingy with men she only started dating, and she thought with her heart more than mind most of the time. "Don't let her bother you. She gets upset anytime something doesn't go her way."

"Phew," he said. "I was afraid you hated me too."

"I don't know you well enough to hate you." And from what I did know, there wasn't a bad bone in his body.

"Well, she was all over me. She wanted to go to bed, but I wasn't feeling it. So, I told her the truth and walked her to her door." He shrugged. "I thought I was being a gentleman."

"I think she's just upset because she was really into you."

"Even so…I don't deserve to be called an asshole."

I was mortified. "Again, I'd try to forget about it if I were you."

"At least you're on my side."

"I never said I was on your side," I said with a laugh. "I'm just telling you what I know about her."

"No, you're on my side. I can tell." He pulled the kabobs off the grill and killed the gas. "These look delicious. They'll go great with the wine." He set the small table on the patio and we began to eat.

I sat directly across from him and cut into my food. The waves crashed in the distance and washed away all the stress I felt earlier in the day. It was difficult to care about anyone or anything when you were in a peaceful place.

Kyle watched me from across the table. "What do you think?"

"It's delicious."

"Thanks. I'm not the best cook, but I can grill."

"The peppers are cooked but still a little crunchy. That's how I like them. And the meat is well done but still juicy."

"Can you cook?"

Saturday

"I cook all the time." I stirred my glass of wine before I took a sip. "I prefer eating at home than eating out anyway. After a while all that heavy food gets to me."

"I know what you mean." He ate his plate quicker than I did then watched me finish mine. The light was fading away, and his face was beginning to disappear in shadow. But I could still see the outline of his cheeks and his lips. Like orbs, his eyes glowed. They were blue like the ocean, giving me that same relaxed feeling.

When I was finished, I sipped my wine and tried to ignore the intense look he was giving me. When we first met he did the same thing. He stared me down openly, piercing me so hard he could see into my soul. Without thinking, I drifted over to him and assumed he was the blind date I'd been set up with. Something about his presence comforted me, made me feel at ease. The kind of feeling was rare for me so I just went with it.

And even now I still felt it.

I didn't know what it was or why it affected me so much, but it was there nonetheless. My natural defense mechanism was to ignore it, to pretend it wasn't happening.

Kyle seemed to be in tune with my moods, because once I felt a new level of discomfort he backed off. "I'll clean these up." He grabbed the dishes and carried them into the house.

When I had my personal space back, I felt more at ease. Somehow, he made me comfortable and uncomfortable at the exact same time. I finished the rest of my wine before I followed him back inside.

Kyle eyed the clock on the stove. "Well, it's getting late. I guess I should head out." He watched my expression like he hoped I would reject.

I didn't feel comfortable sleeping in the same house with a stranger, even if he did seem perfectly nice. It didn't settle with me right and I wouldn't be able to get any moment of sleep if I knew he was there.

"Or I could stay here if you don't mind."

I did mind—immensely. "Uh, I think we should stick with our original plan." He probably wanted to stay here because it was his home—it had nothing to do with me. But even a locked door wouldn't make me feel safe.

Despite his disappointment, he nodded. "That's fine. Do you want me to show you around?"

"No, I think I got it covered."

"My room is the best one in the house. I recommend you sleep there."

"Okay."

He still remained rooted to the spot. He leaned against the counter with his arms across his chest. I'd be lying if I said I wasn't attracted to him. He was the most handsome man I'd ever seen in real life. When I thought he was my date I was actually surprised by my luck. And the fact he was so sweet and thoughtful just made him more desirable. I understood Florence's heartbreak when he ended their relationship at the second date.

But nothing would ever happen.

Kyle still didn't move and it didn't seem like he intended to leave anytime soon.

Now I didn't know what to do. A part of me wanted him to stay, but a bigger part of me wanted him to leave. I couldn't ask him to leave again, not without sounding like a bitch. It was his place after all. If I really wanted to get out of the situation, I'd have to go.

But Kyle recognized my limit once again. "You'll be fine here alone? I can show you how to use the alarm."

"Yeah, that'd be nice."

He guided me to the wall near the door and told me the code to arm and disarm it. "You know where to reach me if you have any trouble. There's a car in the garage if you need to go somewhere—keys are hanging by the door."

"Thanks."

He opened the front door and gave me one final look. "I'll be back in the morning. And my mom's place is literally right down the road. I'm just two minutes away."

"Thank you. Good night."

His eyes were glued to my face, searching my eyes and then my lips. Seconds passed before he finally walked out. When he was gone, I locked the door and set the alarm. His absence comforted me. I was no longer alone in a house with a man I hardly knew.

But his absence also made me feel lonely.

Saturday

CHAPTER EIGHT

Kyle

Mom just got engaged, but she couldn't care less about her new diamond ring, her fiancée, or her trip to Italy. All she cared about was me. "So...a woman is staying at your place?"

I hadn't even brought my bag to my old bedroom yet. "Yeah. I'll be heading back tomorrow."

"Who is this woman?" Mom was certain I was going to spend the rest of my life with Francesca. She really liked her, even after she left me for Hawke—the first time. But when she left the second time Mom despised her.

"I'm hiring her to design my new beach house."

"Beach house?" she asked. "When did you decide on that?"

"At the very last second," I said. "Honestly, it's just an excuse to talk to her."

"My son doesn't need an excuse. You're the most handsome, smartest, and sweetest bachelor in this country. If you want a girl, all you have to do is tell her."

She was a little biased sometimes. "She's a little more complicated than that."

Mom rolled her eyes. "Why do you always like the complicated ones?"

I shrugged. "I wish I knew. Then I would stop." But I really wanted this girl. I didn't have a concrete reason, but that made me want her even more. It wasn't just her beauty or her intelligence. It was so much more than that.

"Why is she sleeping there alone?"

I didn't talk about my personal life with my mom, and for the most part she didn't ask. "She didn't feel comfortable with me being there."

"Is she a prude or something?" she blurted.

I chuckled. "I don't think so. But we hardly know each other. We just met a week ago."

"For most of my girlfriends, a week is too long."

Now we were getting into dangerous territory. "Anyway...I'll go back in the morning."

"Can I meet her?"

Now that would definitely scare her off. "Not this weekend. But maybe some other time."

Mom got that look on her face, like she wasn't happy with the way things were turning out. After Francesca, she was deeply protective of me. She stuck her nose in my business and even tried to set me up on dates with the local debutants. "Greg and Laurie's daughter just moved back here from California. She's a very sweet girl."

"I'm sure she is, Mom." I headed to the stairs so the conversation would end. "But I'll find the right one on my own. She's out there—somewhere."

And I suspected she was right under my nose.

***

"How'd you sleep?" The house was exactly as it was before I left.

"Good. Your bed is very comfortable."

"Thanks." I wish I could have been sleeping in it last night—with her. She wore cut-off denim shorts and a white halter-top, looking like a beach babe. She looked great in everything, from evening dresses to pants. She could shave her head and still look amazing. "I'm glad you had a comfortable stay. It was the least I could do since you came all the way out here."

"It was my pleasure, Kyle." She retrieved her suitcase and placed it beside the door. "Should we get going?"

I tried dragging this trip out as much as possible. If we spent enough time together, maybe she would soften up and agree to dinner. I was one of those guys that loved the chase, but I only loved it for so long. It was clear from the beginning attaining Rose would be difficult, if not impossible. But I wouldn't stop until I got at least one date out of her. "How about we stop for breakfast on the way? I'm starving." I had breakfast at my mom's because she forced it down my throat, but I could eat again.

"Uh, sure." Rose was still committed to making the trip strictly professional. But she behaved differently toward me than she did everyone else, including her friend Florence. She was partially comfortable around me, always making eye contact with me when she avoided it with everyone else. I had hope there was something else there—that she felt what I felt.

"Great. Let's hit the road."

***

It was hard not to be offended that she didn't want me in the house last night. I had to stay with my mother and be interrogated all night long. But I also understood the request. She didn't know me very well and she was just cautious.

But it ruined my plans.

Sitting on the couch together in front of a roaring fire could have kindled a romance. One thing could have led to another, and maybe we would have spent the night together. The chemistry was there, that was certain. But she wouldn't allow it to happen. She didn't have a boyfriend so what was her hesitance?

"Where's your place?" I reached the city along with the traffic.

"You can drop me off at my office."

I hid my irritation at her need for secrecy. "Are you sure? Your suitcase is pretty heavy."

"I'll manage." She looked out the window.

The logical part of me knew I should throw in the towel. She may be into me, but she didn't want anything to come from it. She kept walls of concrete erected all around her so nothing could get inside.

But I couldn't give up.

Saturday

When we reached the office I pulled up to the curb. "Thanks for coming out. I appreciate it."

"No problem. I can promise you, this house is going to be beautiful. You can trust me to do a great job." Her face always lit up when she talked about her architectural designs. Very few people loved their job the way she did. She clearly adored it.

"I'm sure I can." If she were any other woman I would touch her hand or place my hand on her thigh, some kind of move. But she would detest that. I could tell. All I could rely on were my words. "Let's have dinner on Friday night."

I did it. The words were out there hanging in the universe. I kept my confidence high without being too pushy. A gentle smile was on my face, trying to lure her in.

She reached for the door handle and gripped it. "Uh, to talk about the project?"

Now I knew what her answer would be. "No. I just want to spend time with you." This was the time when I would lean in and place a gentle kiss on her lips. But I knew that would just drive her away. I had to restrain myself and rely on my words to seal the deal.

She gripped the handle so tightly her knuckles were turning white. Instead of being excited she looked terrified. "Uh, that's very sweet of you to ask, but no thank you."

No thank you? Who says that?

"I'll talk to you later." She got out of the car as quickly as possible. Flustered, she slammed the car door behind her and the impact shook the car slightly.

Ouch.

She walked to the rear of the car and knocked on the truck.

I stared at her in the rearview mirror, digesting the rejection. I struck out hard. I chewed my inner lip, trying to mask the disappointment. Rejection wasn't something I experienced very often, and now I was getting it at a time when I really didn't want it.

I wanted her.

I knew I should let it go but I couldn't.

I had to try again.

I got out of the car and came to her side. With a click of a button the trunk popped open.

She stood beside me, her eyes downcast and her body tense.

I grabbed the suitcase and carried it to the sidewalk. It was heavy for a day and a half trip.

"Thank you..." She pulled out the handle and prepared to leave.

"Hold on." I didn't block her path, but I steadied her with my voice.

She turned back to me, clearly uncomfortable.

"When we first met, I thought there was something here. In that restaurant...did you feel something?" Was I the only one who felt the ground shake below my feet? Was I the only one who felt time stop? Was I the only one who died inside just to come back to life?

That wasn't possible.

She had to feel it too.

Rose looked into my eyes just the way she did on that night. Her hazel eyes were a brighter color under the light of the afternoon sun. Her full lips were slightly parted, revealing the tip of her front teeth. Even in the tensest moments she was painfully beautiful.

"Rose?"

"I think you're attractive, Kyle. But that's as far as my feelings go..."

My eyes narrowed on her face, searching for a lie.

"I told you I don't date very often, and only when I absolutely have to. So, I'm not interested in anything more."

"Why?" I had no right to ask the question, but it just slipped out.

She looked at the ground for a few seconds before she lifted her gaze. "I prefer to be alone."

I didn't believe that either. There was something she wasn't telling me. "I'm just asking for dinner. That's all. I don't expect anything, Rose."

"You're a sweet man, but my answer is still no." She grabbed the handle and prepared to walk away.

I didn't want to let her walk away. I wanted an answer, a concrete one. Women came and went in my life, but I hardly felt something more than fondness and physical lust. Francesca was the first woman I wanted to be with all the time, and that occurrence was rare. Now I felt that feeling again, but it was a million times stronger—and I hardly knew her.

That meant something, didn't it?

"I really wish you would give me a chance, Rose. Whatever happened to you, I can fix it. Whatever happened in your past doesn't mean anything to me. I can be what you want me to be." I was bending backwards for this woman, laying my heart on the line when she wouldn't even give me a first date. I was swimming against the stream and doing backflips just for an opportunity.

"Maybe it's best if we don't work together anymore."

Fuck. Now I really screwed things up. I pushed too hard and lost my only outlet of seeing her. "I don't want that. You're the best person for the job and I trust you'll make my vision a reality." That was total bullshit, but I couldn't tell her the truth.

That I couldn't let her go.

Hesitance shined her eyes, like she couldn't decide if she should continue our business relationship.

If I didn't do something now I would lose her forever. "I'm sorry I came on a little strong. But when I saw you walk into that restaurant, I thought I felt something—something more than physical attraction. I thought there was some kind of connection there. But clearly I was wrong. I won't bring it up again. This business relationship is important to me and I can't afford to lose it. I'll back off."

She searched my eyes for nearly a minute before she began to relax.

"I would love to be your friend—if you'll have me." I extended my hand. I wasn't looking for an excuse to touch her. It was an experiment. Would I feel something when we touched? Or would there be nothing there like I hoped?

She eyed my hand before she took it. Her fingers clasped around mine and she gave it a gentle squeeze. On the surface, it was a platonic handshake, a business agreement between two partners.

Like last time, the heat traveled up my arm. It burned me from the inside out, giving me the kind of addictive pain I couldn't shake off. My heart skipped a beat just like last time, and my lungs forgot how to take a breath. The fire burned hotter once we came into contact, quickly turning into an inferno.

Her delicate breathing immediately became irregular, and I saw her swallow the lump in her throat. Her lips were parted again, and the fear was in her eyes—the fear of getting burned.

Whatever I felt was still there—and she felt it too.

Saturday

CHAPTER NINE

Kyle

Rose was difficult, unattainable, and simply infuriating.

She wouldn't give me a chance for whatever mysterious reason, and I didn't like that one bit. I wasn't the perfect man, but I did my best to be as close to perfect as possible. I was always respectful to everyone I met, I treated every woman like a queen, and I had a good heart.

That wasn't enough for her?

I wish I could read her mind, discover all her secrets and find out what her problem was. My irritation didn't come from entitlement. I didn't expect her to be with me, but I wish I understood why she didn't want to be with me.

I should throw in the towel and give up. Other women wanted me, would love to have dinner with me, and it would save me the constant headache that pounded behind my eyes.

But I still wanted her.

If I were going to pursue this I needed to talk to Will about it. He only went on two dates with her, but if I kept up this game, I needed to be honest about it. If I did get Rose, I'd have a difficult time explaining my actions.

We were hitting the weights together at the gym. We usually spotted for one another, and right now he was doing bench presses. He bent his elbows at the right angle and lowered the weight to his chest. Then he raised it again, going slow to maximize the use of his muscles.

I stood over the bar with my fingers underneath the metal, prepared to take the weight if I had to. "One more, man."

He did the final rep then racked the bar. He was breathing hard and out of breath, his arms feeling like lead.

"Good job." I racked the weight.

"Thanks." He wiped his forehead with a towel.

I used to go to Crunch Fitness, the same gym Francesca went to, but when she left me, I moved a few blocks over. If we kept running into each other, it would just make it difficult for me.

But now that I was over her I missed my old gym. The equipment was newer and the place was bigger. Sometimes I thought about moving back, but that would be a lot of work.

"I'm going to be so sore tomorrow." He drank his water then returned it to the ground. He hadn't left the bench.

I took the seat beside him. "Me too."

"We should hit legs tomorrow."

"Good idea." I was dreading this conversation, and I thought having it here would be ideal. Other people were around so it wouldn't escalate into a fight. Also, he was tired from lifting so he may not care as much as he normally would. "I want to talk to you about something."

"What?"

"I hired Rose to design my new beach house in The Hamptons."

"You're building a new beach house?" he asked in surprise.

"Yeah, my dad left me the land a few years ago, but I didn't get it until recently."

He rolled his eyes. "I really hate you sometimes."

I got that a lot. "Anyway, Rose and I have been working together."

"Yeah? Did she say anything about me?"

"No..." I hoped this wouldn't blow up in my face. "Honestly, I'm into her. And I'm pretty sure she's into me too."

"What makes you say that?"

I couldn't describe it in a way anyone else would understand. "I can just tell."

"Where are you going with this?"

"Well, I was going to go for her. I just wanted to give you a head's up."

"You're going for my girl?" he asked incredulously.

Anger coursed through me at lightning speed. I didn't like the possessive way he referred to her, especially since it was clear Rose never had any interest in him. "You went out twice, man. And all you did was shake her hand."

"You're still breaking the pact."

"Not really." He was just irritated she preferred me to him.

"Then why are you asking for my permission?"

"I'm not. I'm just letting you know what's going on."

"What about Florence?" he asked. "I thought you were into her?"

When the hell did I say that? That woman was way too bossy and controlling for me. "She's nice but not really my type. Honestly, when Rose walked in, she was all I noticed."

"Obviously," he said. "That woman brings hot to a new level."

I wanted to grab a weight plate and slam it into his skull. Those excessive comments were really getting to me, starting to make my brain boil. "Don't talk about her like that."

"What?" he asked. "All I said was she's hot."

"And knock it off." She was a lot more than a hot piece of ass. Even if she wouldn't let me see through her layers I knew there was a whole ocean underneath her skin.

He rolled his eyes. "Chill out. It's not like she's your girlfriend."

But she was mine. "Anyway, are we okay?"

He shrugged. "I really liked her."

They hardly spoke during their time together. He didn't know her, not like I did. "Not every date works out. That's just how life is. I'd really like it if you were on board with this. I don't want to sneak around."

His eyes showed his irritation, but that look was slowly disappearing. "It looks like you've already made your decision, and if she likes you too, I'm not going to get in the way of that."

"Thanks." Now the dilemma was over with.

"Does Florence know this?"

Since our last date went to shit I hadn't talked to her. "No. I ended our relationship last time I saw her."

"But she was really into you. I doubt she's going to be cool with Rose dating you."

Since Rose wouldn't say anything to her anyway, I should be fine. "We'll cross that bridge when we come to it."

***

A week had come and gone, and I wanted to see Rose.

I had to go about this carefully. If I moved too quickly, I'd scare her off again. I had to use my lawyer expertise to manipulate her into the exact place I wanted her to be.

I called her and tried to stay cool.

"Hello?" She answered with an alluring voice. It was deep but feminine at the same time. The sound was so attractive I forgot that I called her altogether. I sat on the phone, treasuring the echo of her words until my mind stopped playing it.

"It's Kyle. Is this a good time?"

"Yeah. I'm just at work. What's up?" Her voice lacked an edge, so she seemed to have dropped our last conversation from her mind. Since I hadn't called in over a week she had a false sense of security.

"I was wondering about the progress you've made on the house."

"I've been working on it a lot, actually. I have a lot of great ideas." Like always, her voice picked up when she spoke of her passion.

"That's great. Can we get together and talk about it?"

"Sure. I'm at the office now."

"Can we talk over lunch?" I asked. "I've been so busy at work I haven't had a chance to grab a bite."

There was a long pause over the phone.

I hoped she'd take the bait.

"Sure. I haven't eaten either."

Yes. "How about a burger? Mega Shake is just around the corner from your office." It was my favorite burger joint in the city. It started in Seattle then opened in Manhattan. It was a hole in the wall, but the food was unbelievable. A casual place like that was better than a fancy restaurant—at least for her.

"I've been there. It's pretty good."
"Great. I'll see you in thirty minutes."
"Alright."

***

I got there first and waited by the front door. Since I knew she was coming, my nerves were getting to me. She was the first woman to make me nervous, to make me think about every word I said before I actually said it.

A guy covered in tattoos walked inside then stood beside me, waiting for someone. He looked my age. Tattoos of every color covered his arms, and on his left hand was a tattooed wedding ring. He pulled out his phone and read a text message before he shoved his phone back into his pocket.

I couldn't look more different in comparison. I was wearing a suit because I just left the office, and I didn't have any ink anywhere. As a lawyer, it may not go over well.

He turned to me, his blue eyes friendly. "Waiting for someone?"

"A girl."

He chuckled. "I'm waiting for my wife. She's late to everything."

"Aren't they all?"

"You said it, man." He glanced at his phone again. "But she's so damn hot I don't care. That woman can walk all over me and I won't say shit about it." He rubbed the side of his neck before he returned his phone to his pocket.

I didn't know what to say to that so I said nothing.

"I'm Slade, by the way." He shook my hand.

"Kyle. Nice to meet you."

"Right back at ya."

The door opened and a blonde woman walked inside. She had a tiny frame, but her stomach was distended past her hips. She was pregnant, probably six months along. A glittering ring was on her wedding finger, and when she looked at Slade her eyes lit up in the same flawless way.

Slade leaned toward me. "That's my lady. Hope yours shows up soon."

"Me too."

He patted my shoulder then walked toward her. When he reached her he wrapped his arms around her and gave her a kiss that wasn't appropriate for the public. "Missed you."

"Missed you too."

He kissed the corner of her mouth before he took her hand and got in line.

Would I ever have that someday? I never felt so much jealousy for a stranger before. He had a woman who loved him the way he loved her. And they were starting their own family.

The doors opened again and Rose walked inside, lighting up the room the second she appeared. Her hair was curled like last time and it trailed over one shoulder. She wore skin-tight jeans with a blue blouse.

When she saw me standing off to the side she came to me. "Hey. Sorry I'm late."

"You're fine." My natural instinct was to examine her from head to toe, but I kept myself under control. "Hungry?"

"Very."

"Let's get in line." I walked up to the register just as Slade grabbed a tray of food. He glanced at Rose then turned his look back to me. He gave me a dramatic wink before he wiggled his eyebrows.

I chuckled.

He walked to the table where his wife was sitting.

Rose didn't notice the exchange. She ordered the food then grabbed her tray.

I didn't bother trying to pay for her things. She would get uncomfortable all over again. It was best just to do things her way until we reached a new level of closeness.

We sat together in a booth in the corner. On the table was a folder of paperwork, probably full of designs she was about to show me. I took a few bites of my burger and kept my eyes down because I didn't trust myself. I had a bad habit of staring at her.

"How's work?" she asked.

"Good. But the office never sleeps."

"Do you work long hours a lot?"

"Not really," I said. "I oversee the office and take care of all the paperwork. I'm usually there in the morning."

"You don't take cases?" She ate one fry at a time, eating slowly.

"I do but rarely."

"That must be nice."

"I usually advise the other guys on their cases and take care of other things. And I golf too."

"How do you decide what cases to take?"

"It's the ones I'm particularly passionate about. When I'm emotionally invested, I work a lot harder and I do my job to the best of my ability. I don't even sleep most of the time."

"Are you a prosecutor or a defendant?"

"Prosecutor—I put fuckers behind bars." Whenever I thought about the cases I worked on, it made my blood boil. The things the women had to go through were unforgivable. Sometimes I couldn't even sleep because those stories haunted me. "I would never defend a criminal. I don't care how much they pay me."

She held a fry in her hand but didn't take a bite.

I realized I let my emotion get to me and made the conversation awkward. "Sorry...I got carried away. I apologize for the language."

"It's okay. It didn't bother me." She took a bite of her burger but kept her eyes glued to me the entire time. "You sound like a good lawyer. And we need more of those."

"All the guys at my firm are great. I know they care about their cases and the people they represent. They're passionate in the same way, and they don't stop until they get justice for their clients."

She continued to eat, but her mind was still intrigued by my words. "How does that affect you?"

"What do you mean?"

"When you're that invested do you ever really move on?"

I shook my head. "No. Even when I win my cases and get my clients justice, I still feel like shit. I feel terrible the crimes were committed at all. You can never erase the past. You can never take back the things that already happened. And my clients will always carry that."

She looked down at her fries and picked at them. She didn't take another bite, her mind somewhere else.

"Sorry, I didn't mean to bum you out."

"It's okay," she whispered. "What do you do when you lose a case?"

"I don't know. That's never happened."

She looked up again. "You've never lost a case?"

"No." I didn't give up. I pushed on until I got what I wanted. "But I don't take as many cases as the rest of my employees."

"That's impressive..."

"I have a good relationship with a lot of the judges, and I have a good reputation. I think that helps a lot."

She returned to eating her fries, moving at a snail's pace.

Saturday

When I asked her to lunch, I wanted to have good conversation, not drop my work drama on her. We were already off to a bad start. "How's work been for you?" I sipped my soda as I watched her.

"Good." She opened a ketchup packet and squirted it on top of her fries. "Work has been good for a while now. A few years ago, I couldn't get anyone to give me a chance because my company is small and I'm the only employee."

"Good for you."

"I've had a lot of high profile clients, and I know that helped."

"Like who?" My curiosity got the best of me.

"Well, Justin Timberlake wanted me to design his house in Colorado. That was pretty cool. Who else...?" She looked away as she tried to think. "Oh, Chris Martin had me design his beach house in Malibu. Madonna has a place in Connecticut, and I designed that for her."

Wow, she wasn't kidding. "That's incredible."

"They really helped my business a lot. Most of referrals are from word of mouth. I don't spend money on ads or anything like that."

"That's so cool."

"Thanks." Her cheeks tinted slightly. "It's been an incredible experience."

The fact she was an independent business owner made me more attracted to her. Running a business was difficult, and no one else understood that unless they did it themselves. The fact she was a one-woman show was all the more impressive. "Your parents must be proud of you."

She looked down again. "Yeah..."

I hit another touchy subject. Now I had to steer away from it. "What do you do for fun?" It was the first question that came to mind.

"I like to jog," she said. "Usually at sunset in the park."

"That's cool."

"It helps me relax. By the time I get home, I'm exhausted and ready for bed."

"Perfect. Sometimes I can't sleep at night." My mind wandered to work, family, and relationships. By the time I stopped thinking about everything, it was three in the morning.

"A glass of wine always helps."

I wasn't a big fan of wine. Otherwise, that would be an easy solution. "I'll give it a try." I'd finished my food so now I had nothing else to do but look at her. It was my favorite hobby so I didn't mind in the least, but I knew it put her on edge. I held my soda and fidgeted with it just so I had something to do. "Where did you go to school?"

"Here in New York. What about you?"

"The same. I grew up in the Hamptons, but I've been here for my entire adult life."

"Did your father accumulate all of his wealth? Or did you come from a wealthy family?"

"My grandfather was the president of Wells Fargo. And his father before him was the president as well. So yes, I did come from a wealthy background. But my dad made his own way in life. I always looked up to him. That's why I became a lawyer."

"That's sweet."

"I remember my first case. I was nervous as hell, but he guided me through it. I learned a lot from him. He was the greatest lawyer I've ever known." He was passionate about his work and never accepted anything less than the best. When he passed away, it was devastating to my mother, but it was also devastating to me. He wasn't just my dad but my best friend.

"I try to appreciate the time I had with someone rather than focus on their absence. Sometimes it helps…sometimes it doesn't."

I wondered whom she lost. But I didn't ask because she would have given up that information voluntarily if she wanted me to know. "It's been so long that I've had time to move on and accept it. But there are days when I struggle, mainly on the anniversary of his death or Christmas."

"The holidays are hard…"

"Definitely." My soda was empty, but I kept fidgeting with it. I wanted to stare at her without blinking, but she wasn't giving me the opportunity. I would do anything to have that, to be able to look at her all I wanted.

"So, let me show you what I have so far." She opened the folder and took out her sketches. "Let me know what you think."

Saturday

CHAPTER TEN

Rose

Kyle's new home was so much fun to work on. Remodeling existing buildings was much more difficult because I had to accommodate the structure as well as the foundation. Not every change was possible. But designing something from the ground up was a different story.

I had full reign.

Spending time with Kyle gave me a better understanding of his personality. He was laid back and mellow, and he was personable. He could walk up to a complete stranger and strike up a conversation about anything. He was warm and inviting, the kind of person you immediately viewed as a friend.

I really liked him.

When he asked me out I forced myself to say no. He seemed like a catch, the kind of guy women only saw in their dreams, but I knew I couldn't have him. Anytime I started walking down that road, my past would catch up with me. Then the breakdowns would occur, one by one.

We could only be friends.

When he backed off and realized I wouldn't change my mind, everything felt more comfortable. I didn't have to keep my guard up every second of our interaction, and we finally started to feel like friends.

That was all I could handle.

When I completed the rough draft of his design, I texted him. I finished it. Let me know when you're ready to look at it.

I'm ready now.

You want to stop by the office?

The three dots appeared before he answered. How about we get a drink instead? It seemed like he never wanted to be in my office. Maybe it was too small for him. Or he just didn't like the atmosphere.

Sure. We can do that.

McCormick's?

I'd been there a few times. Sure.

I'll meet you in 15 minutes.

***

He was already there when I walked inside, sitting in a booth with a beer in front of him. He wore a charcoal gray suit with a cream colored shirt underneath. His dark brown hair was slightly curly at the ends, and it was messy like he'd been running his fingers through it all day. His jaw was covered with a layer of hair from not shaving for the past few days.

I noticed every detail.

His eyes stood out no matter what color he wore. He was painfully beautiful, almost unreal. He had thin lips that looked kissable. His knuckles were defined and hard, like he had strenuous hobbies outside the courtroom.

When I first saw him in that restaurant, I was taken aback by my attraction to him. It'd been so long since I'd felt arousal for any man. Actually, it'd been years. But he brought my body to life just by his appearance alone.

I didn't think that was possible.

He spotted me when I walked inside, and his eyes were glued to me instantly. He stared at me a lot, and I was growing used to it. Whenever he looked at me he didn't stare at my chest, hips, or stomach. They were always focused on my eyes, giving me nowhere to hide.

Like always, my throat felt dry.

My hands were warm.

And my breathing became labored.

I hoped he didn't notice.

I approached his booth and slid into the seat across from him, the folder tucked under my arm. Now was the time for me to say hi, but being face-to-face with him was unnerving. I cleared my throat because my tongue was awkwardly placed in my mouth. There was no way I could possibly say anything.

His forearms rested on the table, and his cuff links glittered in the light. They were the image of the England flag. He stared at me openly, not blinking. The bubbles in his glass still floated to the top and the foam was heavy. It was clear he hadn't taken a single drink.

And the staring continued.

I wanted to say hi, but now I couldn't remember if I already had. My nerves were getting to me and my throat went dry all over again. Now I desperately needed water— preferably wine.

Kyle moved one hand to his jaw, his fingers lightly resting on his lips. The intense look he gave me was unnerving but not necessarily in a bad way. His heated looks were becoming more common, and now he didn't bother looking away anymore. He stared endlessly, seeing something in my eyes.

My entire body felt hot. The sweat formed under my arms and I crossed my legs just so I had something to do. The folder was placed on the table, and I could easily open just so I had something to look at.

But I didn't.

Minutes passed and neither one of us spoke.

Kyle didn't seem to notice everyone else in the bar. People talked quietly from their tables, while others yelled at the game on the TV. But he didn't seem to care about anything in that room besides me.

The waitress came to our table and broke the tension. "Can I get you something?"

Like a knife, she sliced right through the moment. The tension had built to a crescendo and it couldn't escalate any higher. If it did, I wasn't sure what would happen. Thankfully, she was there. "I'll take a glass of white wine. And some water." With lots of ice, please.

"Coming right up." She walked away, returning us to our strange isolation.

Kyle lowered his hand to the table, revealing his bottom lip and jaw. "Thanks for meeting me."

"Sure." My voice came out a little shaky even though I tried to hide it. He was good at seeming calm. I was terrible at it. "I worked on your suggestions and came up with a new idea."

"Great." He still didn't touch his beer. "How are you?"

I was expecting him to ask about the drawings, and I couldn't hide my surprise when he didn't. "Good. I had a bad fall in the park, but other than that, I'm okay." I twisted my wrist and showed the scrape along my arm.

His eyes moved to the injury, and he immediately reached out and grabbed my wrist, twisting my arm so he could get a good look at it. His fingers trailed along the area in a soothing way, making the inflammation die down for a moment. "I'm sorry to hear that. You should put a bandage on it."

Feeling his hands on me wasn't intrusive like I thought it might be. Actually, it felt nice. "I had one earlier, but it must have fell off." I cringed at the idea of a dirty bandage sitting somewhere in my office.

E. L. Todd

"I'll get you one." He slid out of the booth immediately and walked to the bar.

I didn't even have a chance to protest.

After he retrieved the bandage along with my water and wine, he sat down and grabbed my arm again. "What happened?" Instead of holding my wrist like he had before, he interlocked his fingers with mine and pivoted my arm so he could get a look at the scab. With a single hand he placed the bandage over the wound.

I watched his face the entire time, watching the way he concentrated on his movements. "An ice cream cart was nearby, and the guy started ringing the bell. I stopped paying attention to where I was going and smacked right into another runner. Thankfully, he wasn't hurt."

"I'm glad you weren't hurt worse."

"The ice cream guy gave me a free popsicle because he felt bad for me…"

"Or because he thought you were cute." He applied pressure to the bandage so it would stick. Then he finally released my arm and pulled his hand away.

But his other hand was still locked to mine. His fingers rested on top of my knuckles, and they were warm and inviting. Some of my skin was dry and calloused, just like most men.

I stared at the affection and felt my heart sink into my stomach. I liked his touch—but I also hated it. My natural response was to pull away but I didn't.

"What kind of popsicle was it?"

My eyes darted back to his face. "Pineapple."

"Good flavor. Personally, I like coconut."

"It sounds like we both like tropical flavors."

"Have you ever been to Hawaii?"

"I can't say that I have."

"You can't get pineapple like that anywhere else in the world." His fingers gently rubbed against mine, massaging me. He acted like the touch was completely natural, like we've done it before.

When I felt the heat flush my body and travel to places it hadn't been in so long, I pulled way. Both of my hands fell into my lap, the one place he couldn't reach them.

Kyle didn't move his hand, and he didn't seem offended that the affection was over. In fact, it didn't seem like anything happened at all. The same intense look was still on his face—and it was directed at me. "Did you do anything this weekend?"

"Just worked on your project. You?" I could feel the heat in my face, and I hoped my cheeks weren't red.

"I played basketball with a few friends. Other than that, I stayed in."

"That sounds nice..." I didn't know what else to say.

"I haven't been going out lately."

It was a strange thing to say.

"And I haven't been dating either."

Again, I was speechless.

He glanced at my wine. "How is it?"

I grabbed the stem with shaky fingers and took a drink. "Good." I couldn't truly savor the taste because I was so nervous.

He finally took a drink of his beer. "Mine is a little warm."

Probably because it'd been sitting there for so long. I grabbed the folder and opened it.

His hand moved on top of it, keeping it closed. "What's your favorite restaurant in the city?"

My fingers still gripped the corner. "I don't know...I love everything."

"You don't have a particular preference?"

"I guess I like that Italian place we went to a few weeks ago."

"I liked it too."

"What's your favorite place?"

"Honestly, Mega Shake."

"But that's not a restaurant." That was a glorified diner.

He shrugged. "You like what you like, right? I'm not big on fancy restaurants. It takes forever to get your food, and they never give you enough of it. I find myself more hungry when I leave than when I got there."

"Because you're a big guy."

"Big guy?" he asked. "I hope you mean that in a complimentary way." With his eyes still fixed on mine, he moved the folder to the opposite end of the table where I couldn't reach it.

"I do." I'd never seen him in anything but a long-sleeved shirt, but the definition of his muscles was still obvious. He was tall, at least six two, and he had the most beautiful eyes in the world.

"That's what I was hoping for." He grabbed his beer and took a long drink before he set it down.

Now I knew this meeting wasn't friendly. It'd quickly developed into something more. When he asked me out the first time, I was terrified. But now that I was there, it didn't seem so bad. He didn't make any moves to touch anything more than my hand and we were in a public place. I didn't feel threatened.

And a part of me liked it.

"Can I ask you a personal question?"

When he made me feel like this, it was hard to say no. "Sure."

"When was the last time you were in a relationship?"

It was so long ago I couldn't even remember. "Maybe four years ago."

"Wow. That's a long time."

It seemed like a lifetime ago.

"Did something happen to him?"

"No." It was an odd question to ask. "We went our separate ways. To this day, we're still friendly."

He nodded, but his eyes narrowed in confusion.

"What about you? I know you said you were almost engaged, but was there someone before that woman?"

"No." His eyes lacked any emotion. "There was no one special in my life before Francesca. I'd been looking for a long time before I found her. Unfortunately, she was destined for someone else."

Saturday

"Destined?"

"Even when they were broken up, she said he was her soul mate."

That was intense. "Do you believe in that sort of thing?"

He considered my question for several minutes before he answered. "Never really thought about it. What about you?"

"No." It sounded like something people made up to be romantic.

"Have you ever been in love?"

"Me?" I asked in surprise.

"Yes. You." His eyes were glued to my face so there was no one else he could be addressing.

"No." I didn't have much faith in humanity to begin with. I couldn't picture myself ever loving someone. It was simply impossible.

"Haven't found the right guy?"

"I guess." And I wasn't looking for him. Our conversation remained serious the entire time. I'd never been so intimidated and comfortable at the same time.

He drank his beer again then wiped the foam from his lips.

I thought about kissing those lips, tasting the beer on my tongue.

And then I freaked out.

Why did that thought come into my mind? Where did that feeling come from? Why was I pressing my thighs tightly together? "Well, I should get going...work never sleeps."

He grabbed the folder and pulled it to the middle of the table. "You need to go over this with me."

I had to get out of there before things escalated. I was already having the kind of thoughts I shouldn't. Kyle seemed like a great guy, and I was beyond flattered he had any interest in me, but this was dangerous. I had to stomp out the fire before it got too big. Then it would never die down. "I'm sure you can look it over yourself." I slid out of the booth and quickly tossed cash on the table for my drink. "Let me know your thoughts."

He didn't chase me or look disappointed. In fact, he didn't seem surprised at all. "I will."

"Have a good evening." He leaned back in the booth, his powerful shoulders looking appetizing. He possessed the strength of a Roman soldier, and he had the looks of an underwear model. Even though he didn't want me to leave, he didn't ask me to stay.

"You too."

Saturday

I walked out of the bar and felt his gaze penetrate into my back the entire way. It burned me, making scorching holes that burned all the way through. I didn't need to glance behind me to check.

I just knew.

CHAPTER ELEVEN

Kyle

I needed help.

Women was a subject I knew a lot about. I practiced them just how I practiced law. I had the looks, the charm, and the success. Saying this made me look like an ass, but it didn't make it any less true.

I always got what I wanted.

But Rose kept slipping out of my grasp.

Every time we made progress she slipped away, right out of my hold. When we got close together, she took a step back. Nothing I said or did sealed the deal. Her walls were so high that I couldn't scale them.

I was losing the battle.

It probably wasn't the best idea, but I called Florence because I was desperate. She seemed to know Rose pretty well, and if I could get the right information out of her, it would make my life easier.

She walked inside the restaurant, wearing a skintight dress that was so short it almost showed her goodies. She wore way too much make up, so much it actually looked blotchy, and her hair was bigger than every porn star's in the industry.

She sauntered to my table with forced confidence. It was obvious she thought this was a date, the kind where I asked for another chance to be with her. She was sadly mistaken.

"Hey." Her voice was clipped and aggressive. She thought the ball was in her quart. She assumed I was wrapped tightly around her finger.

I could tell what kind of woman she was. She wanted a man to obsess over her so she could control him, make him pine over her every second of the day. She demanded respect but refused to give it. When she grabbed me and dragged me around she acted like she was entitled to do it.

Not my kind of woman.

Women had a lot more power than they realized, and all that power was in their words. They could ask for anything and get it—as long as they were nice about it. But to push me around and take advantage of my sensitivity was unattractive.

"Hey." My tone was polite but not too polite.

"I knew you would call me." She flipped her hair over one shoulder and tried to look sexy, but she failed miserably.

She was nothing like Rose. "How are you?"

"I've been good. You know, seeing a lot of guys." She grabbed the menu and refused to look at me.

Good for you. "I'm glad you're well." I expected her to ask me the same question in return, but she never did.

"So, what do you want?"

"I thought you knew I would call you?" She could try to play the game all she wanted, but she would never win.

She smiled to herself and kept looking at her menu.

I sipped the wine I ordered and thought of Rose. I was doing this so I could have a real chance with her. Unless I had the information I needed I would never get anywhere. "I've been working with Rose on my new beach house. She's talented."

"Very. She's such a geek."

Geek? "I wouldn't say that."

"She is," she said. "Instead of going out, she prefers to stay home all the time. If it weren't for me she would never go out."

"Maybe she enjoys being alone." I'd prefer it to her company.

"She's too shy. I bring out the best in her." She finally set down her menu and faced me head-on.

"I think she's perfect the way she is." I was starting to suspect Florence wasn't a good friend at all, just a glorified bully.

"That's your opinion." She took a drink of the wine I ordered.

"Is there any particular reason why she's shy?" I felt deceitful going behind Rose's back to get my information, but I didn't know what else to do. She clearly didn't trust me—or all men. If I knew why, I might be able to get into her good graces.

"She's just had bad experiences with men. It's nothing personal."

"What kind of bad experiences?" I hated myself for asking, but it slipped out.

"It doesn't matter." She looked at the menu again.

At least Florence was loyal enough not to spill her friend's secrets. "As a lawyer, I might be able to help her. I've been in a lot of different kinds of situations."

"Then you should tell her that."

She wasn't giving me anything. "When was the last time she'd gone on a date?"

"Why do you keep asking so many questions about her?" she snapped.

"Curious. She's designing my new home."

"I don't see what her personal life has to do with that." She set the menu down again. "I want garlic bread as an appetizer."

Her voice was starting to annoy me. She was bossy and rude, attributes I despised. I couldn't get through this entire dinner with her. My head would explode. "The truth is, I'm very fond of her. I've wanted to ask her out, but she's brushed me off a lot. I'm a good guy and have nothing but respectable intentions toward her. If you could give me some advice, I'd really appreciate it."

Her eyes widened to the size of golf balls. "Excuse me?"

I knew I said the wrong thing.

"You ask me out so you can sleep with my friend?"

"I didn't ask you out, for one. I just invited you to dinner. And secondly, I don't want to sleep with your friend. I just want to get to know her better. She's closed tighter than a clam."

"You're such a pig."

"What?" I asked. "There was no chemistry between you and me. It's not like I slept with you and never called you again. You're treating me like a criminal when I didn't do anything wrong. The second I saw Rose I felt something, okay? That doesn't make me a bad person."

"You're an ass." She jumped to her feet and threw her napkin down.

I stood. "I'm sorry if I hurt your feelings. I didn't mean to." Even though she insulted me left and right every chance she got. "But I really care about Rose—truly. I'm not a man looking for an easy lay. I want something with her—something more. I know she has feelings for me, but she won't give me a chance. If you care about your friend, you should help her."

"Go fuck yourself." She spit on my face then marched out of the restaurant.

I tried not to gag when I felt her saliva on my cheek. It was one of the most disgusting experiences of my life. I grabbed the napkin from the table and wiped it away, feeling everyone's stare on my face.

Saturday

CHAPTER TWELVE

Rose

The second I answered the phone Florence was screaming. "You will not believe what that piece-of-shit, Kyle, did to me."

Kyle? Was she talking about a different Kyle? "What Kyle are you talking about?" Since my Kyle didn't have a mean bone in his body, she must be referring to someone else.

Wait. Did I just call him my Kyle?

"The asshole that I went on a date with. The one you're working with."

What could he have possibly done? Florence was bad-tempered, but she didn't scream like this very often. "What'd he do?"

"He asked me out again."

He asked her out? He told me he wasn't dating anyone.

"So, we're sitting at dinner and all he talks about is you. He asks every question you can possibly think of. I refuse to give up your secrets, so then he asks why you're so withdrawn all the time."

He asked about me?

"Then he said he's really into you and thinks you're into him. But you won't budge." She screamed into the phone again. "Can you believe that? He asked me out just to get to you."

At first, I was touched he was working so hard to get a date out of me. He even went to Florence, someone he couldn't stand, just to figure out how to make it work.

But then the rage set in.

He went behind my back and tried to get answers out of my friend, stuff that I kept private. When I refused to answer his questions, he snooped around anyway. I didn't like that one bit.

"Rose?"

"Sorry...that was a lot to process."

"He's such a pig. I can't believe I actually liked him."

"Yeah..." I was in a daze, still considering everything she said.

"You better not go out with him—ever."

"I wasn't planning on it."

"You should drop him as your client. He's creepy and obsessive. I don't trust him."

Even now I didn't dislike him. I was flattered he hadn't given up when he could pick up someone else in a heartbeat. All he had to do was walk into a bar and he would find someone.

But he kept trying.

"I needed to give you a head's up. Kick him in the nuts when you see him."

"I'll try."

***

I jogged in the park just before sunset. It was my favorite time of day. The sun set over the horizon, blocked by some of the skyscrapers of the city. The light filtered through the trees and gave some respite from the heat.

I listened to a lot of different music when I ran. Sometimes it was pop and sometimes it was R&B. Right now, it was Shakira. "Hips don't lie…" I sang under my breath as I jogged, counting the miles I trekked. My finish line was always the ice cream stand. Perhaps it was counterproductive, but I always wanted a treat after exercising.

I turned the corner than slowed to a walk. I wore leggings with a bright yellow t-shirt so everyone could see me down the path. Other people passed me on the trail, usually walking in pairs.

When I turned to the ice cream cart, I saw a familiar face.

"Hey." Kyle rose from the park bench and walked toward me, wearing running shorts and a t-shirt. His shirt was damp with sweat, and there were still beads on his forehead. Somehow, he looked sexy as hell after exercising.

I looked disgusting. "What are you doing here?" Since I was flustered, I blurted out the first thing that came to mind. For a second I forgot about the conversation I had with Florence. All I thought about was the way his powerful chest looked in his shirt. He had nice calves, and his arms were even better than I pictured.

"Decided to go for a jog. When I passed the ice cream cart, I thought I might run into you."

I was still breathing hard, Shakira playing in my ears.

Kyle heard the song through the ear buds. "Hips don't lie, huh?" He grinned from ear-to-ear.

I yanked them out and paused my music. "Sorry...you just surprised me."

"I hope in a good way."

I still wasn't sure.

"How about we get some ice cream? I'll try the pineapple and you can give the coconut a taste."

I wiped the sweat from my forehead and then tried to fix my hair. I knew I looked terrible, and that made me self-conscious.

Kyle picked up on it. "You look cute. I like the sporty look."

"Yeah right."

"I'm serious." He put his hands in his pockets and didn't come any closer to me.

I felt his unnerving stare and knew I was getting sucked in all over again. "I should get going—"

"Come on. Let's get some ice cream." He cut me off and got in line.

The simple solution to this was to walk away. I didn't have to stay there. I wasn't being forced against my will, and I had the privilege to do whatever I damn well please.

But I stayed.

Kyle paid for the ice cream bars then handed me the coconut flavor. "I'm telling you, it's delicious." He immediately walked down the path at a leisurely pace, licking the popsicle from bottom to top.

I drifted to his side, my feet doing all the thinking at this point.

"How many miles do you run every day?"

"Six." I put the cold ice cream in my mouth and savored the taste.

"Wow. That's impressive."

"You should see my feet. They're covered in blisters and my toe nails are falling off."

"Yikes. The sacrifices we make, huh?" His eyes were on the path in front of us, and he stared at the surroundings as we walked.

"I talked to Florence." It was going to come up eventually. May as well get it over with.

"I figured." He kept eating his ice cream like he didn't have a care in the world. "I'm sure I came off pretty bad."

"You did."

"I know she's your friend and everything, but you of all people understand what she can be like. Keep that in mind before you pass judgment."

"I do know what she's like." She could be difficult and overdramatic, but I still loved her. "I've been dealing with it for a long time now."

"Then you'll give me the benefit of the doubt."

"Fine." I held my ice cream without eating it. "Did you ask her personal questions about me? Why I'm so closed off? What happened to me in the past?" If he lied I'd know about it. I didn't think Florence would make that up.

He sighed before he answered. "I did."

Now my anger flared up. "If there's something I wanted you to know, I would have told you myself. How dare you go behind my back and stick your nose where it doesn't belong. How would you feel if I did that to you?"

He stopped walking, a grim look on his face. "If someone did that to me, I wouldn't like it one bit. In fact, I'd be pissed. But it's different with you. If you were the one asking the questions, I wouldn't have minded in the least."

"What? I'm practically a stranger to you."

"How?" he asked. "I feel more comfortable around you than anyone else. I don't need to know you for years to know what I feel. And call me crazy, but I think you feel the same way."

I stepped back, surprised.

"Tell me I'm wrong." The ice cream was beginning to melt down his hand so he tossed it in the garbage.

I held my own because I was too shocked to do anything else.

"Tell me, Rose." He stepped toward me, getting closer than he ever had before.

I felt my heart race in my chest, about to give out any moment. When he was this close to me, I couldn't think straight. My head was in the clouds. "You're wrong…" The words sounded half-assed even to my own ears. It didn't matter if I was comfortable around him or not. This could never go any further.

Kyle stared at me like he didn't believe a word I said. "I don't believe you—even for a second."

I took a step back, unable to stand in his shadow. "Kyle, you need to back off. I mean it."

"I didn't mean any harm." He dropped his threatening tone, turning docile. "I want you, Rose. I thought if I understood your reservations better I could convince you to give me a chance. That's all."

"Well, I don't appreciate it."

"She didn't tell me anything so your secrets are still safe. And I apologize for what I did."

I wanted to be angry with him, to hold a grudge and march off. But I couldn't. It was impossible to stay angry. "Don't do it again."

"I won't."

"And don't ask me about it either."

"You have my word."

"And leave me alone."

The hurt in his eyes was unmistakable. "That I can't do."

"You don't get much of a choice in the matter."

"Actually, I do. If you didn't feel anything for me, then I would walk away. If I knew you really didn't want me, I'd leave you in peace. But I know that isn't the case. You feel exactly what I feel. There's not a doubt in my mind."

It didn't matter what I felt. It wouldn't change anything.

"All I'm asking for is a date. Please."

"Kyle—"

"Come on. I'm a nice guy that will treat you right. If you gave me a chance, you would see that."

"You're probably right. But that doesn't change anything." I lost my appetite for my treat, so I tossed it in the garbage. Now I just wanted to leave—to forget about this conversation entirely.

Kyle rubbed his temple, showing his frustration for the first time. "Then can I take you out as a friend?"

"What's the difference?"

"There is no difference," he snapped. "But if it makes you more comfortable then we can pretend."

I'd never had a man pursue me this much before, let alone one that had his looks. The more I said no, the harder he pushed. If I said no, he may not give up. He might just push harder. "Why is this so important to you?"

"What?" he asked. "A date?"

"Yes."

He looked away, his eyes scanning the grass beside the path. He considered the question in silence before he turned back to me. "I don't have an answer—at least one that will make sense."

"Try anyway."

His eyes found mine and didn't move again. "When you walked into that restaurant, I knew. What exactly? I don't know. All I know is, there's something here. My heart wouldn't slow down and my body was about to give out. Never in my life have I had that kind of reaction to someone—not even for Francesca. We don't know each other that well, but I'd really love to change that. I think it's what we both need."

I felt the same thing in that same moment. The fact I knew exactly what he was talking about scared me a little bit. When I saw him for the first time, I felt that flutter deep in my stomach. And when I realized Will was my date, I couldn't help but be disappointed.

Kyle studied my face as he waited for a response. "See? You know exactly what I'm talking about."

"It's lust, Kyle."

"Lust?" He spoke like poison was in his mouth and he wanted to spit it out. "I know exactly what lust feels like, and that's definitely not what I felt. It's insulting that you would characterize it that way."

I stepped back, knowing I wasn't going to get out of this.

"Rose, just tell me why."

"Why what?"

"You won't give me a chance. Because I know it has nothing to do with me."

It didn't. In fact, if this were a few years ago, I'd be falling madly in love right then and there. "I don't want to talk about it. Please stop asking." It was one of those things you were ashamed of. I wouldn't tell a soul what happened unless I absolutely had to. It was the worst kind of shame anyone could bare.

Kyle didn't press the topic. "That's fine. But go out with me anyway."

He wouldn't give up. Not now. Not ever.

He stepped closer to me, taking back the distance I put between us. "Rose." He said everything he meant with a single word. That's how well I could read him.

"If I say yes, will you drop it?"

"Drop what, exactly?"

"We go out once and that's it. You'll leave me alone?"

"So, I only have one date to convince you to give me a second one?"

I crossed my arms over my chest and nodded.

"Talk about pressure..."

"That's all I'm willing to give."

He sighed like he was about to scale the tallest mountain. "I like a challenge."

"I have one condition."

"Name it."

"You can't kiss me." That was the last thing I needed. A physical touch was more than I could bear. Handholding was okay, but anything else was too extreme. I knew he would question my strange request, ask me a million questions about it.

But he didn't. "Whatever you want, sweetheart.

Saturday

CHAPTER THIRTEEN

Rose

I gave him my address despite the warning in my heart. Giving out my residence was rare, practically unheard of. But when he asked for it, I didn't know what to say. If I refused, he would just ask me again.

So I gave in.

People weren't always what they seemed, but Kyle seemed genuine. He was thoughtful and caring, and he was confident and protective. It was hard to picture a man like him being anything less than heroic.

But I'd been wrong before.

I wanted him. But I was also afraid of him.

At seven on the dot he knocked on my door.

I wore jeans and a blouse, not wanting to get too dressed up. I didn't know what Kyle planned, and I hoped it wasn't extravagant. This looming date was giving me anxiety and I tried to keep calm. He was a good man and I had to keep telling myself that.

Everything would be okay.

When I opened the door, I saw him standing on the other side. A handful of flowers was in his grasp, an assortment of wild flowers. He wore dark jeans and a collared shirt, getting dressed up but not formal.

That made me feel better.

"I picked these myself. And it took me all day." He placed them in my grasp.

Every flower was different. There was one red rose, a yellow daisy, and a white lily, among a variety of others. The fact they weren't quickly bought at the store was touching. He took time out of his day to pick each one—and that meant something. "That was sweet..."

"I'm glad you like them. I thought about you while I picked them."

I gave him a small smile before I set them on the entryway table.

"I've been looking forward to this for the past few days."

I grabbed my clutch and felt my cheeks redden. Since I didn't know what to say, I didn't say anything at all.

"Thank you for going out with me. I think we'll have a great time."

"I'm sure we will." After all the sweet things he said, I had to say something in return.

He never stepped into my apartment. He always stayed on the other side of the threshold. "Ready to go?"

"I am." I shut the door behind me and locked it. "Where are we going?"

"You'll see." He extended his hand, his palm facing the ceiling.

I stared at it blankly, remembering the last time we touched. He held my hand at the bar, and at the time it felt so right.

He let it hang there, silently pressuring me.

I swallowed the lump in my throat and placed my hand in his.

He smiled in a genuine way, showing all of his perfectly straight teeth. "I have a good feeling about this."

***

We entered an apartment building near Central Park. Judging the lobby, it was a higher end place. The tile was manicured to perfection, and there was even a doorman at the entrance.

My body tensed in fear. "What are we doing here?" I assumed we were going to dinner or bowling or something. "What is this place?"

"This is my apartment building." He walked to the elevator and hit the button.

His apartment building? Did he want to go back to his place? That panic settled in all over again, the same terror I felt when he wanted to stay together at his beach house. There was no way in hell I was doing that. "I have to go." I turned on my heel and immediately ran for the exit. My chest caved in and I could hardly breathe. The world was starting to spin and the nightmare descended.

"Rose?"

I pushed out the front door before the doorman could reach it. When I was at the sidewalk and near other people I felt safer. There were witnesses—tons of them.

"Rose." Kyle caught up with me and grabbed me by the arm. "What's going on?"

I twisted out of his grasp just the way I'd been taught. Then I took my defensive stance immediately, ready to break his nose if I had to. I may be small, but I'd fight to the very end and take him down with me.

Kyle raised both hands in surrender. "Okay...I don't know what's going on here."

"Don't touch me."

He took a step back. "Rose, what's wrong? What did I say? What did I do?"

"I'm not going into your apartment. That's not something I signed up for." I wasn't going to be alone with him, not when I felt this uneasy.

"We aren't going into my apartment."

I hated liars even more. "Oh really?"

"Yes, really," he snapped. "I planned something special for us. And it has nothing to do with my apartment."

"Whatever." I wasn't falling for that.

"Rose, be logical for a second. You really think that I would hurt you? That I have some evil plan up my sleeve?" He lowered his hands to his sides. "You know I'm a good guy. Trust your instincts—not your paranoia."

I lowered my stance, my pulse slowing down. "What is it?"

"Just trust me." He extended his hand just as he did earlier.

I stared at it with no intention of ever taking it.

"Rose, you can trust me. Let me prove it to you."

I eyed the door before I looked back at him.

He kept his hand extended. "You can do this. I know you can."

I knew I was overreacting. Sometimes when I was in uncomfortable situations, the terrified version of me took over. My coping mechanism was to run, to avoid every possibly dangerous situation. But as a result, I wasn't really living. "I'm sorry."

"It's okay." He slowly reached my hand and grabbed it. "Come on. I know you'll love it." He guided me to the door and back inside. The doorman eyed us but kept his comments to himself.

We got inside the elevator and Kyle hit the button to the top floor. "I can't wait to show you."

I stood beside him and felt the shift of gravity as we moved to the top floor. My stomach felt weightless for a moment before the elevator stopped. When the doors opened, we looked directly at the roof and the skyline in the distance. The summer breeze moved through my hair, caressing it like the feel of soft fingers. All my fright disappeared when I realized what this was.

Kyle took my hand and guided me further on the rooftop. A table set in the center, underneath a stream of white lights. Silver platters were on the table, covered to keep warm. A bottle of wine was being chilled in the bucket with two glasses beside it.

Kyle pulled out the chair for me. "It's a beautiful night, isn't it?"

"It is." I sat down and felt him push my chair in.

He took the seat across from me and poured the wine. "I'm going to be honest. I ordered this as take out and threw it on two plates. So, I hope you like steak."

I removed the lid and inhaled the smell. "It looks delicious."

"I'm sure it's delicious too—because I didn't make it."

"Those kabobs you made were good."

"Thank you. I forgot about that."

As I cut into my food, I felt the humiliation creep in. When I thought he was taking me to his apartment, I threw a tantrum and threatened to punch him on the sidewalk. I caused a scene with the passerby as well as the doorman. It was embarrassing, to say that least. He must think I'm a freak.

Kyle watched my face as he ate, and he seemed to read the distress on my face. "It's okay. I understood why you thought that."

After my behavior he was actually making it easy on me. "I'm sorry I freaked out…"

"It's alright," he said. "Let's just forget about it."

It was hard to when I made such a scene. "I just—"

"You don't have to explain anything." He drank his wine and focused on his food. "Honestly."

Now I understood him even less. Why was he spending so much time trying to be with a woman who obviously had some issues? He didn't seem to care even though he could have anyone he wanted. It didn't make any sense.

"How was your day?"

"Good. Yours?"

"It was okay. I had to step into the office today. Everyone gets paid on Monday so I had to settle the payroll."

"You don't pay someone to do that?"

"No. My dad taught me to manage everything on my own. You can't trust anyone when it comes to that sort of thing. Besides, if I have someone else take care of it, then I'm pretty much handing my company over to someone else. It's mine so I should take some pride in it."

"I can understand that."

"Besides, I need something to keep me busy. Otherwise, I'll golf all day and play video games."

"That sounds nice."

"It is. But too much free time makes me irresponsible. If I'm not busy, I'm not at my best."

"Why don't you take more cases then?"

"I'm selective because it's so draining. Trials don't end in two weeks. There's a lot of planning that goes into it. Sometimes I work so many hours that I really don't get paid much."

I ate my food slowly, feeling my stomach slowly settle after my rampage. Kyle changed the subject to make me more comfortable, but my actions still lingered in the back of my mind. I felt foolish—and stupid.

"Do you ever get tired of designing?"

"No. Not yet, at least." I loved sitting in my quiet office with a pencil in my hand. Time passed so quickly I couldn't process it. Before I knew it, eight hours had passed and my drawing was finally complete.

Saturday

"Are you going to design your own house?"

I laughed because it was absurd. "I'm never going to be able to afford that."

"Really? Why not?"

"I know you have two beach houses, but most of us don't even get one." I drank the wine and felt the cool liquid move down my throat. Once it reached my stomach it felt warm.

"Well, it doesn't have to be a beach house. It can just be a house."

"Building a home is a lot more expensive than buying an existing one. And I could never afford one in the city. That's just unheard of."

"But if you had the opportunity, would you design it?" He ate quicker than most people I know. Half of his plate was already gone, but he wasn't shoveling everything down his gullet. He just took big bites.

"Of course."

"Do you have an idea what it would be like?"

I shrugged. "For the most part. But you can't design something unless you know the landscape first. Otherwise, it's too difficult to picture it."

"I don't have a creative bone in my body. I'm all about logistics and facts."

"I don't agree with that."

"Really?" he asked. "Why not?"

"I'm not a lawyer so I'm not totally sure of this, but I would assume a lawyer has to find different ways of approaching situations. He has to figure out how to change the narrative, to convince a grand jury what they should believe. You have to be somewhat creative in order to do that."

"I guess," he said with a shrug. "Never really thought about it like that."

I looked up at the lights and saw them contrast against the black background. A moth was hovering around the lights, infatuated with the warmth. "Did your mom think it was strange that I stayed at your beach house alone?"

Kyle took a moment to figure out what I was referring to. "Not at all."

If he were lying I would never know.

"She just got engaged so her mind is elsewhere right now."

"She did?"

"Yeah. They've been seeing each other for about a year."

"That's great."

"I like the guy. He has his own wealth, which is a lot more than my mother's, so I know he's genuinely interested in her as a person. And he treats her right. You know, takes her on nice trips, opens every door for her, compliments her...she's happy."

"That's great." I thought he might struggle to accept a new man in his life. Instead of being selfish he was happy for his mother.

"My mom has been through a lot. She deserves to have some joy."

"Do you have other siblings?"

He paused before he took a bite of his steak. Only a heartbeat had passed, but the hesitance was noticeable. "No, I don't." He kept his eyes down after that, not making eye contact with me.

I reached uncomfortable territory so I didn't push any further. "Where's the wedding?"

"I don't know any of the details. I suspect they'll marry somewhere beautiful, have a small ceremony."

"I'm sure it'll be nice."

"Me too." He finished his plate then placed the lid on top so it wouldn't attract gnats.

I couldn't finish mine. I was stuffed to the limit. I felt my stomach protrude out past the top of my jeans. When the food was placed in front of me, I couldn't control myself. I chowed everything down. "I'm so full."

"Me too." He grabbed the lid and covered my plate.

The nighttime air was the perfect temperature. It was cool, but not cold enough that I needed a jacket. A part of me wanted to stay there forever, but another part of me wondered what else was planned for the evening.

"Dessert?"

"I don't know...I already ate too much."

"Come on. You can manage it. I believe in you."

I chuckled. "Thanks for not losing faith."

He left the table and tossed his tablecloth on the surface. "Let's get some ice cream."

"Should we clean this up?"

"No. Someone will take care of it when we leave." He grabbed my hand and helped me to my feet. When I didn't need his help anymore he still kept his fingers wrapped around mine.

I let the touch linger—because I liked it.

***

"Since our last encounter with ice cream ended badly, let's give it another try." He handed the popsicle over then licked his own.

Now that I could enjoy my treat I paid attention to the taste. "You're right. It is good."

"See? What did I tell you?" Casually, his hand slipped into mine again.

I looked down at our joined fingers and noticed how much larger his hand was than mine. It was always warm whenever we touched, and the comfort it brought me was inexplicable.

"Do you think New York will always be your home?"

"I couldn't imagine living anywhere else—especially for work."

"What about LA?"

"Too much traffic."

He laughed. "And you don't think there's traffic here?"

"You can get everywhere on foot. I don't even own a car."

"It's definitely something you can do without. I only have one because of my property outside the city."

"I'll admit, I'm a little jealous of your car."

"Yeah?" He took a few bites of his ice cream, consuming half of it in minutes.

"Yeah. Everyone loves sports cars. The engine is so powerful, and everyone looks at you as you drive by. And you must pick up girls like crazy."

"Of course," he said. "But I don't need a car to do that."

For the first time, when I pictured him with other women, it made me uneasy. Was it jealousy that I felt? Questions came to mind, but I never asked them. If I did, then he might ask me the same ones in return. "You're right. You don't."

"You should take it for a drive," he said. "The next time we visit the property you can be behind the wheel."

"You trust me with your baby?"

"I trust you with anything, sweetheart."

No one ever called me that before. Somehow, he made it sound sweet and sexy at the same time.

"I might not give it back to you."

He chuckled. "I'll just buy another one. Then we can have matching cars."

Now I couldn't tell if he was joking. He had that kind of money lying around? I had a lot in savings and had everything I needed, but I couldn't wrap my mind around that kind of level of rich. "Do a lot of women go for you for your money?"

Saturday

"I don't know if I would say a lot, but I'm sure there's a good number of them."

Florence was obsessed over the fact he was a rich lawyer. Other than his looks, that was all she cared about.

"But I can tell when that's the case. It's pretty obvious."

"Does it bother you?"

"If we're having a fling, no. But if we're dating, yes."

"I'm surprised your mother hasn't arranged for you to marry another rich woman in the Hamptons."

He laughed loudly. "Oh, she has. Believe me."

"You didn't like any of them?"

He shook his head. "No chemistry. I'm not exactly sure what I'm looking for when it comes to women, but I recognize it when I see it." He gave my hand a gentle squeeze.

The heat flushed through my body, burning my toes and fingers.

Kyle tossed the stick of his Popsicle in the garbage can. "Well, that was pretty good. But I have to stick with the coconut."

I tossed mine as well. "That's funny. Because I prefer the pineapple."

***

At the end of the night, Kyle walked me to my door.

My heart was stuck in my throat the entire time, dreading the end of the date. They usually ended with a kiss goodnight, and a possible invitation inside. I told him I didn't want any of that, and he'd probably stick to his promise.

But I was concerned anyway.

He faced me as we stood in front of my apartment, and his hands were tucked deep into his pockets. "Thank you for spending the evening with me. I hope you had a good time."

"I did." It was the best date I'd ever been on. No guy had ever put that much effort into impressing me. It was both romantic and relaxing at the same time. All he did was hold my hand and nothing else.

He glanced at my door before he looked at me again. That intense look was on his face, the same one he gave me in the bar and the moment we met. His eyes were dark, like he was thinking of a single thing to the exclusion of everything else. The look was unnerving because it was so intimate. He stared at me in a way no one else ever did.

Saturday

The hair on the back of my neck stood on end.

He took a step closer to me, closing the gap between us.

My chest heaved with the breath I tried to take. My lungs burned and the acid pooled in my stomach. His proximity terrified me. He said he wouldn't kiss me and he didn't strike me as the kind of man to go back on his word, but I was nervous nonetheless.

His face was close to mine, and the tip of his shoes touched the end of my feet. The scent of his cologne and natural scent washed over me, a mixture of Old Spice and masculinity. His chin had been shaved a few days ago, and the hair was already starting to come back in. His lips were irresistible, thin and soft but so kissable. I hadn't kissed a man in a long time. I couldn't even remember how it used to feel.

I wanted to step back, to put distance between us. But I didn't.

"I'm not going to kiss you." His eyes were stuck on my lips, watching them part in surprise. "Unless you want me to."

I did.

But I didn't.

My throat went dry and I couldn't speak. Kyle made me comfortable, but he also terrified me at the same time. All men did.

"But can we do something else?"

My breathing hitched. "I don't catch your meaning..."

"Can I hug you?"

"Hug me?" I blurted out the words without thinking, saying them with unease.

"You know what a hug is, don't you? The affection shared between friends and family..."

"I just wasn't expecting you to say that."

"Does that mean I can?"

A hug was harmless. It wasn't any different than holding hands. That was something I can do. "Sure."

His hands immediately gripped my waist, feeling the area just below my ribs. He rubbed the area gently before his hands glided to my back. He took his time getting there, feeling every inch of me.

He took a final step, closing the gap between us entirely. His arms wrapped around me, taking up my entire back, and he pulled me against his chest. Without any warning, he placed his forehead to mine, his lips just inches away from my mouth.

Saturday

I'd never had a hug like this before.

He looked down into my face, his eyes glued to my lips. His thick arms formed steel cages around me, protecting me from everyone and everything. His chest felt powerful against mine. With every breath he took, it felt like a concrete wall was pressing against me.

One hand moved up my back, migrating past my shoulder blades and to the back of my neck. His fingers massaged the area gently before they migrated into my hair. He clasped the strands and got a hold of me, keeping me in place.

Now I couldn't breathe.

He gently guided me against the wall and cornered me, giving me nowhere to run or hide. His heartbeat could be felt against my chest. It was pounding hard, matching the same pace as my own. He felt exactly what I felt.

His hand squeezed my back, bunching up my blouse in his fingertips. He never remained still even for a moment. He gripped me tightly in any way he could. His other hand continued to fist my hair, feeling the soft strands against his fingertips.

A quiet moan escaped his lips, almost inaudible.

I tried to control my breathing but I struggled. My body burned with excitement, feeling the energy course through me in powerful waves. I felt alive for the first time in forever.

"This feels so good." His thumb brushed along my cheek and stopped when it reached the corner of my mouth. His rough skin felt smooth against my soft cheek, complimenting each other perfectly.

It did feel good—and that alarmed me.

"I could do this for the rest of the night...and never get tired of it." His lips hovered near mine but didn't move any closer. He kept his word to me even though it was obvious he didn't want to.

But this felt more intimate than any kiss we could have.

He held me just like that forever. Half an hour passed within the blink of an eye, and we continued to stand outside my apartment door without moving. My hand glided up his chest, feeling the hard muscle underneath his collared shirt. When they wrapped around his neck I felt my body have a small explosion. His skin was hot to the touch, and it burned me slightly.

I'd never felt such strength under my fingertips. He was solid, chiseled and hard like marble. When I touched him he didn't feel like a man, but a statue. My fingers clung to his skin because they never wanted to let go.

"I feel it again...that sensation."

I knew exactly what he was talking about. It was the same feeling I got when I shook his hand for the first time. It wasn't physical lust or infatuation. It was something else entirely. An invisible force was binding us together, getting us to grip each other so tightly that our knuckles turned white.

"I know you feel it too."

I knew exactly what he was referring to, and while the sensation made me higher than a kite, it also broke me. Even if these feelings were true and there was something here, nothing could come of it. After the things I'd experienced, he would never want me—not if he knew the truth. And I couldn't trust him anyway—not completely. I was damaged, broken beyond repair, and he deserved something better than that.

It took all my strength to pull away, and somehow I managed it. "I should get going...it's getting late."

His hands released me, but they were tense like they didn't want to let me go. The disappointment in his eyes was heartbreaking. It shattered me with just a glimpse.

"Thank you for dinner. Good night." I got the door unlocked and prepared to dash inside.

"I want to take you out this weekend. I have the perfect place in mind."

"I'm sorry, Kyle." I didn't have the strength to say anything else. Turning him down was already difficult enough.

"Don't do that," he whispered. "Don't push me away."

If I didn't keep a firm hand, I would get sucked in all over again. "I went on a date with you. I kept up my end of the bargain. Now you need to keep up yours." He agreed to leave me in peace if I gave him one date. Now that the exchange had been completed he needed to leave me alone. I knew this was how things would end between us, but I hadn't anticipated how much it would hurt.

Because I did like him.

Kyle pressed his lips tightly together in irritation then he ran his fingers through his hair, trying to think of something to say to change the outcome. "Rose…I know you feel the same way."

It didn't matter if I felt the same way. "Goodbye, Kyle." I walked inside and began to shut the door.

He lodged his foot in the crevasse. "I'm not asking questions you don't want to answer. But I'm telling you I'm nothing like the men you've encountered. I'll never hurt you or cause you any kind of pain. I'm a good man. I promise."

I believed him. But that wasn't enough. "I know you're a good person, Kyle. I can tell."

'Then go out with me again."

"It's more complicated than that. What we had was fun while it lasted, but we need to move on."

"I don't want to move on."

I waited for him to remove his foot. "You promised me you would back off."

He sighed like he hated himself for making that promise to begin with.

"Spend your energy on a woman who deserves you—and appreciates you."

"I would—if there was someone else I actually wanted."

I gripped the door and waited for him to move his foot. Every second this continued, the more painful it became. He was dragging it out, making it more unbearable. "Just let it go."

E. L. Todd

He stared at the ground for several heartbeats before he finally pulled his foot back. The pain weighed heavily in his eyes. He was searching for a loophole, anything to change the situation.

"I'm sorry."

He wouldn't look at me again, too disappointed to meet my gaze. "I am too."

I slowly shut the door and pressed my body against it, feeling the crippling pain wash over me. Kyle was the first man I felt something for. Over the past few years, I didn't think I was capable of feeling anything because I was so numb. But then he appeared and brought me back to life.

But I couldn't keep him.

Saturday

CHAPTER FOURTEEN

Kyle

All the motivation and drive that once burned inside me had disappeared. I didn't care about anything anymore. My body went through the motions of everyday life, but my mind wasn't in it.

I sat at my desk for nearly an hour and stared out my window, thinking of my date with Rose. Everything went according to plan, with the exception of her meltdown. We had a great dinner and got dessert in the park. She allowed me to touch her hand, and she even showed enthusiasm for it.

And that hug.

The affection was PG, but it felt more like Mature. Feeling her body against mine gave me the greatest high I've ever felt in my life. Having her that close to me brought me a strange sense of peace. I didn't feel the anguish from losing my father and my sister. It was like those travesties never happened. Being in her arms felt like home.

I knew she felt the same way, the strong connection between our bodies that made us melt into each other. My fingers burned from touching her bare skin. When they reached her hair I stopped breathing altogether.

It was the most incredible feeling in the world.

But she didn't want to see me again.

She closed the door in my face and walked away. She didn't give me another chance or another date. For her, that was the end. I promised I'd leave her alone after the first date, but I didn't expect her to walk away.

I thought she'd want to see me again.

It blew up in my face and there wasn't a single thing I could do about it. Any logical person would tell me to throw in the towel. If I had to work this hard to get her to notice me, then she wasn't worth it. I was a good guy, respectful and polite. I always did the right thing in any given situation, and my heart was too big for my own body.

But she didn't see that.

I needed to move on and forget about this woman. I needed to find someone who cared for me with the same intensity I cared for them. I deserved a happily ever after, to find the woman of my dreams that would bring me nothing but happiness.

But I still wanted her.

And I knew I would always want her.

Mark walked inside with a folder tucked under his arm. He didn't knock or give my assistant the opportunity to warn me. The redness of his eyes displayed his exhaustion, and the grim look on his lips showed his irritation.

"One of those days, huh?"

"No." He plopped down into the chair. "It's worse than one of those days. Shit, it's the worst day of my career."

Did he lose another case? I told him to take a break when the last one didn't end in his favor. "What's up, man?"

He tossed the folder on my desk. "I had a client a few years ago that was sexually assaulted and raped by a group of guys. Only one of them was identified and taken to trial. Despite all the evidence I had, most of it was circumstantial, and I lost the case."

Why was he bringing this up now?

"It was one of those cases that kept me up every single night. I didn't get justice for my client, and that asshole walked free. I knew he was still out there, possibly doing the same thing to some other poor girl. Losing that case killed me."

"Like I said, you can't win them all."

"Well, I should have won that one. If I had, this wouldn't have happened."

"What wouldn't have happened?"

He glanced at the folder on my desk. "It's the same guy and the same crime—but a different client."

My blood turned ice-cold. My lungs stopped working altogether—and so did my heart. "Fuck."

He stared at the ground, one hand covering the left side of his face. "If I won that case this wouldn't be happening. Now I have another woman with nearly the exact same story. Because of my inadequacy, this happened again."

"That's not true, Mark."

"Yes, it is," he snapped. "I can't lose this case. I just can't."

It was easy to get sucked into these situations because we were so passionate about them. All the lawyers in my office were good people, and they cared about doing the right thing for our clients. Sometimes we got our hearts broken in the process. "You won't."

"I better not."

I opened the folder and browsed through the pages. There were two case files inside, one of the first victim and one of the second. "What are the similarities?"

"Both were bind dates from a dating app. When they got there, it was a trap." That was all he said because he didn't need to say anything more. "This client is still in shock over it. I can't get her to talk. The only information I have is from the police report."

I couldn't blame the woman for shutting down. It was painful enough to go through the trauma. And then to be questioned about it...was difficult. "Give her time."

"I can't give her too much—if she wants me to win."

The girl was a few years younger than I was—brunette and attractive. Her picture showed the bruises and scars on her face. The rape kit also showed five different deposits of semen—with different DNA.

My blood boiled.

"The guy is pretty good-looking. He sets up these dates with cute girls and then charges money for four guys to join in at the end of the night. Shit like this makes me never want to have a daughter."

"It makes me want to commit murder." I wasn't joking. If I could put a bullet in his brain and get away with it, I would. I had no morality when it came to this sort of thing. If he was in the ground, he couldn't do this to anyone else. And that's all that mattered.

I flipped threw her case file until I reached the second one. It belonged to the previous girl, the first victim of the assault. In this instance, there were only two, but I was sure there was more. The other victims probably never got the police involved. No woman wanted to tell the world they'd been raped.

I read through the file and disposition, seeing exactly what happened in that case. Mark did everything he could to get a guilty verdict, but the jury still claimed him as innocent. I noticed there were more men than women on the jury, and that made me sick inside.

I reached the photos in the rear and skimmed through them, seeing the bruises and abrasions on the victim's arms and legs. When I reached the head shot, I froze in place.

The woman had brown hair with hazel eyes. Her face was red and purple from the swelling. There was a cut on her bottom lip, and her left eye was swollen shut. Despite all the changes, I recognized her.

It was Rose.

"Fuck." I rose to my feet, feeling the paper shake in my hands. There was no mistake that it was her. I'd recognize those full lips and green eyes anywhere. I'd been angry a lot in my life, but I never felt this kind of rage. All I saw was red and I wanted to murder the man who did this to her. Not even murder, I wanted to torture him. I wanted to inflict so much pain he begged for death.

And even then I wouldn't give it to him.

"Kyle? Everything alright?"

The paper slipped through my fingers because I couldn't look at it anymore. I couldn't handle the unbearable pain that ripped apart every organ in my body. To my surprise, my eyes were wet with tears. But they weren't tears of sadness.

They were tears of rage.

"Kyle?" Mark watched me with concerned eyes.

"I'm taking this case." I snatched the picture from the floor and shoved it into the folder.

"What? I already worked on the last one. I know more—"

"It's mine." I stared him down, threatening him with my eyes. "End of discussion." I would put this asshole away for the rest of his life. I couldn't afford to lose this case. And frankly, I was the best lawyer in the building. I would use every weapon at my disposal to get justice for this woman—and Rose. I didn't trust anyone else to do it.

I. Will. Win.

***

Now that I knew the truth, everything made sense.

Rose's frightful behavior, her sudden outbursts, and her inability to trust me weren't from paranoia. She had a concrete reason to feel that way. Frankly, I was surprised she went out with me at all.

Knowing she'd been raped broke my heart—literally. Every time I took a breath, it caused me pain. I couldn't think straight because everything hurt so much. She was a beautiful person who didn't deserve to go through that—no woman did.

But it didn't change the way I felt about her.

I still saw her in the exact same light. To me, she was still beautiful and perfect. Her lips still drove me wild, and the brightness of her eyes made me more obsessed. I still longed to hold her, to kiss her—to be with her.

Nothing had changed.

Now I couldn't give up—not when I knew the truth. She did feel something for me, the exact same thing I felt for her. Our emotions were real and true. We could have something incredible if we gave it a chance.

But how did I make that happen?

Should I tell her I knew the truth? Or would that make her push me away? If she knew I knew, would she no longer be able to look me in the eye? Would the shame consume her until she couldn't look past it?

Should I keep it to myself?

I decided to keep the truth a secret—for now. She didn't want me to know the truth to begin with, so acting ignorant would give her the best comfort. She wouldn't think about it when she was with me, and maybe she would stop thinking about it altogether if I waited long enough.

I had to see her but didn't have a plan to make that happen. I could go to her office, but she probably wouldn't leave because she was working. I couldn't show up at her apartment because that would make her uncomfortable.

Understandably.

So, I did the only thing I could think of. I called her.

After a few rings, she answered. Since she waited so long, she probably debated taking the phone call at all. "Hello?" Her deep voice was as beautiful as ever. It washed over my ears in a delicate way, making me think of the beach and the sunshine. I remembered the way the wind blew through her hair as we stood on the deck of my back porch. I remembered the way her beautiful eyes glittered like gems buried deep within the earth.

"Hey, it's me." I stood on the sidewalk, directly in the path of pedestrians. They walked around me, paying no attention to me at all. I looked up at the building, knowing one of the windows belonged to her.

She didn't speak for thirty seconds. "Hey."

I was caught off guard by her beautiful voice again. It brought me so much satisfaction. The experience was strange, impossible to understand. "How are you?"

"Good...you?" She couldn't figure out why I was calling, so her guard was up—like usual.

I felt like shit.

Actually, I wanted to die.

I couldn't believe I could feel this much pain.

Everything hurt—constantly.

"Great." It surprised me how easy it was to lie. But telling her the truth, that I was heartbroken, would only make her feel worse. "I miss you."

She was silent.

I knew she missed me too, even if she didn't say it.

"I miss you too."

Both of my eyebrows rose and nearly jumped off my face. My heart filled with too much blood and could barely pump it out. All my nerve endings were on fire, burning everything into ash. I couldn't believe she said it back. "Can I see you?"

She gave the answer I expected. "Kyle, that date was a one-time thing. We need to walk away and forget about each other."

I could never forget about her. "Do you like funnel cakes?"

Her surprise echoed through the phone. "Funnel what?"

"Funnel cakes. You know, like glorified donuts. If you've never had one, we need to try it. It comes with powdered sugar and chocolate. You'll love it."

"Uh..."

"Come on, let's go. I'm standing outside your building right now."

Her gasp traveled through the phone.

I shielded my eyes from the sun and looked up at the windows. A second later her face appeared.

I waved. "Howdy."

"Why are you standing out there?"

"I wanted to stop by and say hi. That's all." Since we were this far apart she shouldn't feel uncomfortable. If I were standing right outside her door, it would just be creepy.

"If I say no, are you going to come up to my apartment anyway?" The fear in her voice was unmistakable.

And it broke my heart. "Of course not. If you don't want to go, that's fine. I'll leave." I wanted her to spend time with me because she wanted to, not because she was forced to. "But I really hope you come down and join me." I kept staring at her window, watching her distant face through the blinds.

She stepped away from the windows and sighed into the phone. "I told you I didn't want to go on another date."

"Can we hang out as friends?" If I couldn't have all of her, I wanted some of her. "What's the harm in that?" I'd proven myself to her many times, but I kept my patience. After what she'd been through, we could take this as slow as she wanted. I'd jump over every hurdle in my path if she were the prize at the end. "Besides, you've got to eat sometime."

"I don't know if a donut qualifies."

"It's not just a donut. Sweetheart, it's so much more than that. You'll see what I mean."

She still hesitated.

I tried not to take the rejection personally. I knew her restraint had nothing to do with me. "Well, I'm going to have one myself. Maybe we can get together a different time." If I kept pressuring her, it would just make it worse. All I could do was extend my hand. It was up to her if she wanted to take it.

"I'll go."

I kept the smile off my face even though it took all my strength to accomplish that. "Great. I'll meet you down here."

"Okay."

***

We sat across from each other at the table near the window. We both had funnel cakes of our own. Mine was covered with strawberries and strawberry sauce while hers was hidden under layers of chocolate.

She stared at it like it was a beast. "This thing is enormous."

"It's great, huh?"

"There's no way I can eat this by myself."

"Then I'll take care of it." I was only allowed to have a meal like this once a month. If I ate too much sugar, my body would pay the price. "That's what I'm here for."

"There's no way you could eat both of these."

"Is that a challenge?" I rose to every challenge, and I always beat them.

"Not sure yet…" She pressed her fork into the cake and broke a piece off. "Here we go…" She shoved it into her mouth and chewed slowly.

"What did I tell you?" I asked. "It's the best shit ever, right?"

She nodded just before she swallowed. "Wow, you weren't kidding."

"I know my stuff." I ate everything on my plate while keeping my gaze locked to her face. Now I couldn't get the image of that photograph out of her mind, the one where she was covered with cuts and bruises. Anytime I thought about the file, vomit moved up my throat. It was a despicable crime, something that kept me up late at night.

"What have you been up to lately?"

"Just work." I was preparing for my case to go to trial. The justice system didn't have the delivery speed of McDonald's. Cases could go on for months—sometimes years. All my spare time was devoted to creating my strategy. I couldn't afford to lose this case. And society couldn't afford to have another rapist on the street.

"No golfing?" Her lips rose into a smile, and she looked so beautiful when she allowed her natural features to come through.

"No...unfortunately." I wouldn't have time for that for a while.

"Did you pick up another case or something?"

"Actually, I did." I wouldn't go into the specifics to spare her the heartbreak. She didn't need to know anything about it. When I put him behind bars, I would tell her. It would be my gift to her.

"What's this one about?"

She never asked me that before. "I'm not at liberty to say."

"Oh, I'm sorry. You're right."

"It's okay." The fact she asked me anything at all was a good sign. "How's work?"

"Good. But to be honest, I haven't worked on your design..."

Probably because she assumed we wouldn't be seeing each other anymore. "That's fine. I'm not in a hurry anyway."

"That's a relief."

Without asking, I took a bite of hers. "The chocolate is good."

Since I took some of hers, she took some of mine. "Yours is too. But maybe we can split one next time."

192

I tried not to react, but it was difficult. It was the first time she spoke of us having plans in the future. I drank my water to cover up my smile, knowing it might spook her off if she caught the look. "Sounds like a good idea."

***

I wanted to get inside her apartment. If she were alone with me inside closed doors, it would be a great way for her to realize she could trust me. But I couldn't make that happen by my own manipulation.

She had to invite me.

I walked her to her door at the end of the night, dreading the goodbye part. I never knew when I would see her again every time we parted ways, but there was a good chance I would at least get a hug from her.

And her hugs were the best ones I've ever had.

"I apologize for introducing you to the funnel cake," I said. "Now you're going to be addicted."

"The fact it's around the corner from my office doesn't help," she said with a chuckle.

"Have you had crepes before?"

"Crepes?" she said. "Those wraps filled with chocolate and fruit?"

"So you've tried them."

"I know what they are, but I've never had one before."

"Really?" Did she live under a rock? "Well, that's the next thing on our bucket list."

"Yeah, I guess so." She pulled her keys out of her purse, her eyes downcast.

I had to get inside, but I didn't have a clue how to make that happen—unless I forced it. "I had a great time tonight."

"Me too." She got the key in the door and pushed it open, the keys still hanging from the keyhole.

This was tricky. She seemed to be in a good mood, calm and comfortable. If I pushed too hard, I'd lose the moment. But if I didn't try hard enough we'd never move forward. "How long have you lived here?"

"A few years. It's close to work so I like it."

"Cool. Can I take a look?" I kept my hands in my pockets and didn't move toward her, giving her as much space as she wanted. There was no other way to show my intentions unless I said them out loud.

"Uh..." She kept one hand on the door and looked terrified.

"It's okay," I said quickly. "I was just curious to see what your place looked like. It's not a big deal." Too much pressure would make her cave. It was difficult to find that balance, to push her when it was necessary and when to back off when she needed it.

She gripped the door handle, still unsure.

"Good night," I said. "I'll talk to you later."

She pressed her lips tightly together before she answered. "Yeah, you can come in."

She just invited me inside her apartment? Did that just happen? The evening had been going remarkable well. I almost couldn't believe it. "You're sure?"

She nodded.

"Cool." I walked inside, keeping my hands in my pockets. I took a look around her place, seeing the small living room and kitchen area. For an apartment in Manhattan, it was pretty nice. It was bigger than a broom closet, something most people had. "It's nice." It was decorated in earthly tones, suiting her personality and demeanor perfectly. If I walked into this apartment without her present, I would have known it belonged to her.

"Thanks." She shut the door behind her, and her shoulders were rigid. She was hunched slightly in a peculiar way, like she was forcing herself to relax and her body wouldn't obey.

I didn't walk down the hall to take a peek of her bedroom. If anything, that might make her uncomfortable. "Is it okay if I sit down?" I walked to couch and stared at her large TV.

"Of course."

I sat down at the edge and looked at the picture frames on the table. All of them were images of her and her friends, hiking or going to the beach. Florence was in one of them.

"Shit, I forgot my manners." She smacked herself in the forehead. "Would you like something to drink?"

"Water is fine. Thanks."

"I'm sorry. I don't do this a lot..." She turned back and walked into the kitchen.

"It's no big deal." The fact she invited me inside was a big deal. Now I knew she was comfortable around me—and she really did like me. If I were anyone else, she would have shut the door in his face. I really had a chance to make this work.

She set the glass of water on the table. "Anything else?"

"No, thank you." I crossed my legs, resting one ankle on the opposite knee. I grabbed the water and took a sip, trying to act as normal as possible. Being alone in her apartment was too significant to ignore.

She sat down on the opposite end of the couch. "You want to watch something?"

"Sure. What are you into?"

She glanced at the time on her phone. "America's Funniest Home Videos comes on right now."

"You like that show?" I always left it on in the background when I was at home working on briefs.

"Yeah. It's nice to watch something family friendly. Everything else on TV is rated R these days."

"I know what you mean."

She turned on the channel and leaned back, her eyes on the screen.

I didn't make a move to sit beside her. A part of me wanted to grab her hand or place my arm around her shoulders, taking advantage of the situation to have some kind of affection. But I knew it wasn't wise to push the envelope. Just the fact I was inside her apartment was amazing.

She laughed when a dog chased his own tail in a video. He kept spinning around until he got dizzy and toppled over. Her eyes lit up in joy and her face looked natural, poised.

We weren't technically on a date, but it was the best one I've ever had. There wasn't a fancy dinner or a bottle of wine. There wasn't hot sex at the end of the road. It was just she and I— together.

And it was perfect.

***

I was exhausted and sleep deprived. This case was taking all of my focus and it hadn't even started yet. I was obsessed to the point of insanity. My rage and pain edged me forward, pushing me to limits I'd never breached before. Every time I read a new account of the crime, I ground my teeth so tightly together my jaw hurt. Rose had only been in my life for a short amount of time, but I'd become so fond of her that I couldn't comprehend it.

The fact this happened to her—shattered me.

I had to get justice for her even if she didn't know about it. I had to fight for her, to do the right thing. What happened to Rose was in the past and nothing could change it, but I could stop it from happening to someone else in the future.

And I would.

I gave her space for a few days so I wouldn't come on too strong. The last time we hung out it went perfectly. If I pushed her for more, she might cut me off altogether. Besides, I had a lot of work to do at the office. I put in more time than I'd ever had before, determined to win this case with ease.

I got tickets to the Mets because they were playing The Warriors the following night. Since they were her favorite team, I thought it would be the perfect excuse to see her again. She wouldn't say no to a free ticket.

Nobody would.

When five days had come and gone, I called her. It was nearly impossible to downplay my feelings and pretend I wasn't thinking about her all the time. She was always in the back of my mind, but I couldn't reach for the phone and text her whenever I felt like it.

I listened to the phone ring a few times before she answered.

"Hey." It was the first time she didn't answer me in a dismissive way. I didn't detect her walls that time. She spoke to me like I was a friend—someone she trusted.

Saturday

"Are you watching America's Funniest Home Videos?"

"Yeah. How'd you know?"

"I'm watching it too." It was on in the background. At the moment, there was a dog wearing sunglasses at the beach. A bandana was around his neck, with the American flag print.

She laughed into the phone. "He looks so cute with sunglasses on."

I loved her laugh. There was nothing else like it. "Yeah...pretty cute."

"Did you know it's on Netflix? So you can watch every season."

"We'll have to have a marathon."

"Good idea," she said with excitement.

I really liked the way things were going. It was too good to be true. "Are you busy tomorrow night?"

"Depends. Why?"

At least she didn't shut me down entirely. "I have two tickets to the Mets tomorrow. Want to come along?"

"Oh my god. Aren't they playing The Warriors?"

"Yep."

"Yes! Of course I want to come along. How much is the ticket?"

"Not a dime."

"Don't be like that," she said. "If I'm going to take a ticket, I'm going to pay for it."

"I got them for free." That was a lie, but she didn't need to know that.

"How?"

"I know people." Another lie. "It's tomorrow at seven. So, I'll pick you up at six. Is that okay?"

"Absolutely. Oh my god, I'm so excited. I'm actually pacing in my apartment because I can't sit down."

The thought made me smile. Whenever I made her happy, I was happy. "I'm glad you're excited."

"Thanks for inviting me."

"There's no one else I'd rather go with." That comment was a little strong, but it was too late to take it back.

Thankfully, she let it slide. "Alright. I'll see you tomorrow."

Saturday

CHAPTER FIFTEEN

Kyle

When I picked her up, she was wearing a Stephen Curry jersey with a Warriors baseball cap. She looked cute, to say the least. She wore dark skinny jeans under her jersey, and Nike running shoes were on her feet.

"I'm really digging the sporty outfits you wear."

"You don't think people will give us a hard time?" she asked. "You know, because I'm not rooting for The Mets?"

"Who cares?" I asked. "Let's do what we want and worry about it later."

She buckled a fanny pack around her waist and walked out.

I eyed the dark green bag with a raised eyebrow. "A fanny pack?"

"Yeah, they are so convenient," she said. "Hands free." She locked the door behind her and walked down the hall beside me.

I tried not to laugh. It was dorky but cute at the same time.

She caught the look. "What?"

"Nothing."

"You think it's lame?"

"Actually, I think it's cute—on you."

"A basketball game is no place for a purse—or a clutch."

We took a cab to the stadium then walked inside. I got great seats three rows back. We were right behind The Warriors' bench. We'd get a great view of everything—and all the players.

"Shit, these seats are incredible." She'd never been so enthused over anything in my presence. Her eyes were bigger than golf balls, and she took in the scene like it was the coolest thing in the world. "I can't believe I'm here. I've always wanted to come to a game."

"It's pretty exciting." Her happiness was infectious. I liked this side of her—the happy and carefree one. If she relaxed more often every day could be this way. "Want something to eat? A beer?"

"A beer and a chili dog would be perfect."

"Great. I'll be right back." I left the chair and scooted down the aisle.

She opened her fanny pack to get some cash.

"I'm not taking anything from you." I kept walking so I wouldn't have to listen to her protests. She could label it however she wanted, but as far as I was concerned, this was a date.

***

The Warriors won—which was what I was hoping for.

"I can't believe that last shot Curry made." She walked beside me down the sidewalk. We would have gotten a cab on the way home, but the streets were congested with cars. Everyone was trying to get out at the same time. "The ball just flies in there like a magnet."

"It's pretty incredible."

"And it's even more crazy that he does it at the last minute. He literally has one second to prepare for the shot. I swear, it's all muscle memory with him. His body just knows how to play the game. Incredible."

All of people passed us on the sidewalk, talking loudly and drunk from the game. I stuck close to her side so no one would bump into her by mistake. I was listening to every word she said, but I was also focused on getting us out of there. "His dad was a basketball player. He probably learned a lot from him."

"I wish I was good at sports."

"Have you ever tried?"

She shrugged. "Not really. I did dance and ballet, but that's about it."

"You're a dancer?" I could picture her moving across the floor gracefully, wearing tights and a tutu.

"Was a dancer," she corrected. "I haven't done it since high school."

"That's still cool."

"I guess. It's relaxing and strenuous, but not as interesting as watching the NBA."

"Well, you're comparing apples and oranges." The group we were walking with got into an argument. It wasn't clear what they were saying, and within seconds they started pushing and shoving each other, F bombs dropping left and right. A beer bottle was thrown to the concrete where it shattered into shards. Then one of the guys grabbed a piece of glass, prepared to stab the other.

Shit.

I placed my body between Rose and the commotion, and my hand automatically wrapped around her waist. I'd never touched her that way before, but I didn't think twice about it now. I guided her from the commotion, keeping her pressed against me.

She looked over my shoulder as we walked, seeing the violence that started. More men got involved into the fight, and soon the radius increased.

"We're fine." I kept my voice calm even though I didn't feel calm. I had to get her out of there before she had a meltdown. The evening went so well and I couldn't afford a setback. I wanted to put our relationship in cruise control and just enjoy it.

I took her down a different route just to avoid the fight, and after a few blocks we were clear of the calamity.

"What were they fighting about?"

"I don't have a clue." My arm remained around her waist, and I loved the curve of her hips in my grasp. Even though we were just in danger, it was hard to stay concerned when my hands were on her.

"Where are we now?" She searched for a street name.

"I know where we are. We'll just take the long way back to your place."

"At least you know where we're going."

After a long walk we reached her apartment building. A few people were talking in the lobby, wearing Mets gear. We quickly walked passed them and took the elevator to her floor.

When the doors opened the silence descended. My ears appreciated the break. For the last hour they were ringing from all the screaming at the courtside. We walked to her door.

She got the door unlocked. "Thanks for taking me to the game. I had a great time. Actually, I had the time of my life."

My lips automatically rose into a smile. "No problem. I loved spending the evening with you."

She eyed her open door then looked at me. "There are so many drunk weirdoes out right now. Why don't you hang out here for a bit until they go home?"

I could manage on my own. I wasn't afraid of a group of drunken men. The only time I was scared was when I had a lady with me. But I wasn't going to pass up on the offer. "Thanks. I appreciate that."

We walked inside and she turned on the lights to her apartment. The city glowed outside the window, and far into the distance the park was visible. The city was a big place, but it was arranged to maximize space and people. Even if you lived two blocks from someone, there were about a hundred thousand people between you.

"I wonder if we were on TV."

"I wouldn't be surprised if we were."

She opened the fridge. "Do you want anything?"

"Water, please."

She grabbed a bottle and tossed it to me. "Sometimes I wish I lived in California so I could watch them play more often."

"The west coast isn't my place." I took a long drink before I placed the bottle on the kitchen island.

"Why not?"

"Their oceans are so cold. Have you ever been?"

"Actually, I haven't."

"I've been for the firm, and the water is barely above freezing. It's nothing like the water we have here."

"Surely, there must be something you like about California."

"Not really," I said. "The traffic is a nightmare. That's all I ever focus on." I walked to the couch and tried to think of my next move. My arm wrapped around her waist earlier so would she let me hold her hand? Or was I pushing my luck?

She sat on the opposite end of the couch, exactly where she'd been sitting last time. She had a beer in her hands and she took a drink before she turned on the TV. "What should we watch?"

"Well, I know our favorite show isn't on."

She turned on TBS. "The Mummy. Dude, this movie is always on."

My head snapped in her direction. "Did you just call me dude?" My grin wouldn't disappear. When she was herself she said the cutest things. She didn't think before she spoke. Words just came out.

"Well, yeah. But it's true. This movie is always on TV."

"Because it's awesome. It's one of those movies you can just watch—even if it's smack in the middle."

"I know." She set the remote on the coffee table. "I guess we're going to watch it then."

"Fine by me."

She grabbed a blanket from the bin beside the couch and pulled it over her legs. She got settled into the couch and watched the TV, her eyes growing heavy.

Instead of watching the movie, I watched her. My head faced forward and my eyes wondered in her direction. She was the most fascinating creature I'd ever met, and I loved staring at her like this. I wish I could do it when she was aware of it—that would be even better.

***

An hour into the movie, she was fast asleep.

Her cap had loosened and fallen off, and the blanket was pulled tightly against her chest. Her mouth was slightly parted as she breathed. If she were comfortable enough to fall asleep with me in the room, then she didn't see me as a threat whatsoever.

And that made me happy.

She couldn't sleep there all night, so I turned off the TV and scooped her into my arms. She was lighter than I expected, and I loved holding her that way. She fit perfectly against my chest, like she was meant to be there.

I carried her into her bedroom and gently set her on the bed. Her room was small, with one queen size bed and a white dresser. I removed her shoes but kept everything else in place. Then

Saturday

I pulled back the blankets and tucked her in. She didn't stir once—probably because she was exhausted.

Since she was fast asleep I took advantage of her vulnerability and stared at her. Her hair came loose from her ponytail and the strands fell softly around her face. When she was asleep she looked peaceful—like she didn't have a care in the world.

She was beautiful.

My lips burned as I watched her, desperate for a piece of her. I could take this as slow as she wanted, but I was a man and I had needs. All I really wanted was some affection— mainly a kiss.

I let my desire get the best of me and I leaned over the bed. My lips traveled directly to her forehead, and once they were there I gave her a long kiss. My mouth felt right. Her skin was warm and she smelled like vanilla. I wanted to stay there forever, to enjoy the sudden ecstasy that rocked through me.

But I knew I'd overstayed my welcome.

I pulled away and stared at her for another moment, seeing her small chest rise and fell with deep breaths. If I could stay there forever I would, but I knew I couldn't.

I walked out of her bedroom and shut the door behind me. When she woke up, she would wonder how she got into bed. Hopefully, she wouldn't freak out that I went into her bedroom. Obviously, nothing happened so she had no reason to be scared.

Since I didn't want to leave the door unlocked, I lay on the couch and got comfortable with the blanket she left behind. I kicked off my shoes and tried to fit my long body across the cushions but couldn't completely fit. My feet hung off the edge while the TV played in the background.

I could lock the door and slide the keys underneath, but I didn't want to. I was looking for an excuse to stay there, to be there when she woke up the next morning. I was looking for any reason to be with her.

Any reason at all.

Saturday

CHAPTER SIXTEEN

Rose

When I woke up, I realized I was in my bed. I didn't walk there myself, and I certainly didn't take my shoes off. I was carried—by strong arms. The previous night returned to my thoughts and I remembered the last thing I did before I fell asleep. I was sitting on the couch—with Kyle.

I pulled the blankets down and realized I was wearing the same clothes as the night before. My Warriors jersey was still on, and my jeans were on as well. My baseball cap had fallen off at some point.

The anxiety passed when I realized there was nothing to be upset about.

I was fine.

Before walking into the living room, I went into the bathroom to check my appearance.

Just as I feared, my makeup was a mess. The mascara was bleeding all over the place, and my foundation was pretty much gone. No makeup was better than this clown stuff.

I washed my face and patted it dry before I walked into the living room.

Too many sizes too big, Kyle lay on the couch with his feet dangling over the edge. He was an enormous man in comparison to the small furniture. He probably got a terrible night of sleep. One arm was draped behind his head while the other rested on his chest.

It was the first time I slept alone with a man. We were in different places, but we were still in the same apartment. I never meant for it to happen, but it came to pass anyway.

But nothing happened.

I walked to the kitchen and got a glass of water, trying to be as quiet as possible.

Kyle must have heard the refrigerator door because he sighed then sat up. He rubbed the sleep from his eye then fingered his hair. For just waking up, he looked undeniably handsome. The sleepy look in his eyes was somehow sexy. Not too many people could pull that off. "Good morning." He eyed me hesitantly, like he expected me to do something upsetting.

"Morning." I put on a pot of coffee. "Would you like some?"

His chest automatically deflated with ease. "Sure."

I grabbed two mugs and listened to the pot make its usual noises. The water boiled from within, making a loud rumbling noise.

Kyle leaned against the couch and continued to rub his eyes like he couldn't wake up. "How'd you sleep?"

"Good. You?"

He eyed the couch with a sarcastic grin. "It's not quite as comfortable as my bed…"

"Why didn't you go home?"

"I didn't want to leave the door unlocked all night. And I didn't want to wake you up." He rose to his feet then brushed the wrinkles out of his clothes.

I watched the way his shirt fit to his body. It wasn't tight, but it fit snugly against his chest. The definition in his torso was obvious even when he was clothed. I could see the distant grooves of his pectoral muscles. His arms were just as strong, as if he threw tree logs around for sports. "How do you take your coffee?"

"Black."

I poured two mugs and handed one over.

He sat at the kitchen table and drank it slowly, the steam rising from the surface and making the apartment smell like morning.

I sat next to him and added a splash of cream and sugar. At one point in time, I didn't trust Kyle at all. When he took me to his apartment building, I jumped to the worst possible conclusion. And when he took me to his beach house, I made him leave because I couldn't stand the idea of being alone with him. But now I made it through the night with him just in the other room. Was I getting better? Or was Kyle just an exception?

"Do you have any plans today?"

"No. I need to wash my bedding since I slept in the same clothes I wore to the arena." I cringed in disgust. I wasn't the most hygienic person, but I was particular about the bed I slept in.

He chuckled. "Yeah, that's true. You have a washer and dryer in here?"

"Yeah. Down the hall."

"That's convenient."

"Do you?"

"Yeah. But I know how rare that is." He drank his coffee until the glass was empty. "Thanks for the fuel."

"No problem."

He placed the empty cup in the sink then gathered his phone and wallet from the table. "Well, I should get going. I'm in desperate need of a shower."

The disappointment washed over me and I wasn't sure where it came from. I hadn't expected him to stay, but I didn't expect to depart right away. Normally, I couldn't wait to get away from any man I was near, but now I found myself dreading his absence.

It was a strange feeling.

Nothing could ever happen between us because I simply wasn't capable of it, but I loved being with him. He made me feel comfortable without even trying. He always made me laugh, and he even made me feel safe.

He was my best friend.

"Okay." I did my best to keep the sadness out of my voice but some of it slipped through. Without making eye contact I walked to the door and acted natural, bottling up the letdown. I was beginning to scare myself, disliking this attachment that came out of nowhere.

Kyle met me at the door, but instead of walking out, he looked me in the eye. That usual intensity was there. He stared me down like he had every right to do so. The look no longer haunted me. Now it was so common that it was strange when he didn't do it. My mouth went dry like it always did, but now it felt right. My breathing picked up and I suspected he noticed. "Unless you want me to stay."

I held his gaze but didn't respond.

"Because I will if that's what you want."

He had the unnatural ability to pick up on my mood, to read my thoughts even when I wasn't sure what I was thinking. He knew things about me without asking any questions, and he seemed to understand me even though he knew me for a short amount of time.

"I want to stay too—but only if you want me here."

I couldn't bring myself to say the words out loud. A part of me was ashamed of my answer. I was beginning to need him, to want him beside me all the time. If he knew the truth about the things that happened to me he wouldn't want me. I was wasting his time and his hopes, but I couldn't stop myself. It was nice to feel at ease around someone, to trust someone like this. "I want you to stay."

***

"What do you think this one is about?" Kyle stood beside me in front of the painting. We spent the afternoon at The Museum of Natural History, something neither one of us had ever done despite living in the city our whole lives.

"Uh…" I tilted my head to the side like that would help. Getting a different angle could make a difference. But the colors and images still blurred together without significance. "Herding cattle…?"

He chuckled. "I guess that could be it."

"What do you think it is?"

"Your guess is as good as mine," he said with a shrug. "I think they're firefighters trying to spray down wild animals with firehouses."

I definitely didn't see that. "That's an idea…"

"Too bad they don't have the answers posted on the wall."

"That would make it too easy."

We moved onto to the other paintings in the museum, looking at the different artwork that didn't make sense to either one of us. Some of the portraits of significant figures were beautiful, and a lot of the handmade pottery was fascinating as well. But neither one of us understood abstract art.

Saturday

"What do you think this is?" Kyle stood in front of a display of metal balls. They were dispersed around a metal base, looking random and strange.

I eyed the title. "The Tale of Time."

"Well...that title didn't help."

It seemed like a random creation, with different balls hovering around. None of it made any sense.

"I could totally be an artist," he said. "I could throw my garbage together and auction it off to the highest bidder."

"It seems that way, huh?"

He walked around the display, looking at it more carefully. "Do you think they are planets?"

"Could be." They were all spherical spheres. "But it can't be our universe. They aren't placed correctly."

"No..." He leaned forward to get a better look. "This one is Saturn—look at the rings. That's Jupiter because of the granular surface. But you're right, they aren't in the correct locations."

I was still lost.

He considered the situation like a mathematical problem. He rubbed his chin as he remained deep in thought. Then when he had the answer he snapped his fingers. "It's the beginning of time, when the planets exploded in the Big Bang and stretched outward across the universe."

That made sense to me. "I think you're right."

"That's why it has that title."

Another clue. "Good point."

He flexed his biceps. "I win."

"I didn't realize it was a competition."

He gave me that cute smile, the one that reached his eyes. He had such a handsome face, and it really showed when he had that grin on his face. "Not a close one, at least."

***

We decided to get sandwiches for lunch, so we sat across from each other at the deli just down the street. We shared a bag of chips while we discussed the museum.

"Could you make a design for a building and submit it as art?"

The question sounded like a joke, but since he said it seriously I knew it wasn't. "Depends on what the building is."

"Couldn't it be anything? What if you made a real-life model of the whole city? I think that would be pretty cool."

"Sounds like a lot of work."

"I'm sure you'd get paid for it."

"Eh." I wouldn't be compensated appropriately for all the hours that would require. It would be a donation of my time, something I had very little of anyway.

"Eh?" he asked with a laugh. "You're Canadian now?"

"No, it was just the best response."

"Eh."

I chuckled and threw a chip at him.

He opened his mouth and caught it like he'd been expecting it. "Thank you. Now I can eat hands free."

I eyed his thick sandwich, layered with turkey, ham, and roast beef. "You think you can catch that hands free?"

He shrugged. "Eh."

"Oh my god. Stop making fun of me."

"What?" he asked innocently. "It's fun. And it's so easy to do."

"When the tables are turned you won't like it very much."

"There's nothing to make fun of me for. I'm awesome."

I rolled my eyes.

"What? You don't think I'm awesome?"

I tried to stop myself from smiling but I couldn't. "Eh."

He laughed before he took another bite of his sandwich.

A quiet companionship fell over the table. As time passed, I grew more comfortable around him, but now it reached an all-time high. It seemed like we'd been friends all our lives, that we knew each other better than anyone else. I wasn't self-conscious about what he wanted from me. I didn't think about that horrible night four years ago. I was at ease—I was happy.

More people filed into the deli, the bell ringing overhead. I couldn't see anyone who walked inside because I was facing the opposite way, but that damn bell told me everything I needed to know.

Kyle glanced at the door then did a double take, like he saw someone he recognized. He immediately looked down at the table, hiding his face and his attention. He kept eating like nothing had changed, but his body language said otherwise.

"You okay?"

"Yeah, I'm fine." He ate a few more chips and kept his head down.

I glanced over my shoulder and saw a group of girls. There were four of them, and they were all the tall and beautiful type. Their hair was done to the point of perfection, and their makeup was good enough to make an appearance on TV. If I spent that much time dressing myself up I'd never leave the house. It'd be bedtime by the time I was finished.

One of the girls stared at Kyle, and when her eyes widened in recognition, I knew she knew him.

I quickly faced the other way and tried to act like I wasn't staring.

Heels echoed behind me, and within seconds she appeared. "Kyle."

Kyle looked up when he realized he'd been spotted. "Hey, Cassandra. How are you?"

"I've been better," she said coldly. "I haven't heard from you in a while." She turned to me and gave me a cold look. Then she turned back to him.

I felt uncomfortable—even a little sick.

"I've been busy." Kyle stopped eating and focused all of his attention on her. He gave her a look that wasn't cold, but it wasn't inviting either. "It was nice seeing you, Cassandra. Have a good day."

She pressed her lips tightly together in a scowl. "When you call me, I won't answer."

"Well, that works out," he snapped. "Because I won't be calling you."

Her mouth gaped open, appalled. "You're such an ass."

"Thank you."

She flipped her hair so hard her neck almost snapped. Then she marched off, her hips shaking dramatically. Instead of ordering, she pulled her girlfriends out of the deli and left.

Kyle stopped eating, clearly losing his appetite.

I didn't ask any questions because the exchange was pretty clear. Kyle obviously dated her, probably slept with her, and then walked away. Jealousy coursed deep inside me, but I had no idea why it was there. I had no right to feel anything.

Kyle finally met my gaze. "I went out with her a few times before we met. She didn't mean anything to me."

"You don't have to explain yourself..."

His eyes never left my face. "It was mainly a physical relationship. I lost interest after a week or so."

I ate a chip just so I had something to do.

"I haven't seen anybody since we met." He said that already, and now he was repeating himself. "I just want you to know that."

My cheeks felt warm so I kept my gaze averted, unable to look him in the eye.

Kyle kept staring at me, waiting for me to look up.

Since he was waiting for a response I gave him one. "Okay."

"Are we okay?"

"Yes, Kyle."

He reached across the table and rested his fingers under my chin. He touched me in a way he never had before. His fingers were gentle as he forced my chin up, making me look him in the eye.

My throat suddenly went dry.

His thumb slowly moved up my chin until it rested on my bottom lip. He kept it there, letting his warm touch linger. His eyes stared at the area, infatuated with the appearance of my lips. He looked at me again, a serious look in his eyes. "Are we okay?"

I nodded, unable to say anything coherent.

"Okay." He dropped his hand and leaned back in his chair, putting distance between us.

I was relieved his touch was gone, but I also missed it at the same time.

***

He walked me to my door, wearing the same clothes he'd been wearing since yesterday. He showered at my place so he looked his best. But he could roll around in a puddle of mud and still look his best.

I stared at the door and was surprised by the feelings deep inside me. I didn't want him to leave—again. We'd spent the last twenty-four hours together, and I wasn't tired of him. Cassandra made me jealous, but she didn't put a wedge between us.

"Thanks for spending the day with me."

I should be thanking him. I was the one who asked him to stay. "I had a great time."

He put his hands in his pockets, something he usually did when we were alone. "I did too."

I couldn't invite him inside. That would be too much time together and he might get the wrong idea of what we were. I wasn't even sure how I felt at this point. It wasn't smart to rush it.

"Do you want to get dinner on Wednesday?"

I was glad he wanted to see me again, but I was disappointed it was so far into the future. That was four days away. It seemed like an eternity.

"That case I picked up has taken a lot of my time." He must have spotted my sadness. "I've got a lot of dispositions to get through, evidence review, and everything else you can think of."

"Of course. That should take priority."

He pulled his hands out of his pockets and took a step toward me, closing the distance between us. Like they had a mind of their own, his hands moved to my hips and squeezed me gently. His forehead pressed to mine and he closed his eyes as he held me.

I felt myself drift away, like I was on a cloud high in the sky. His touch brought me so much comfort that I couldn't fathom it. It used to terrify me, make me squirm with unease. But now it felt right.

His arms locked around my waist and he pulled me against his chest, my face resting against his beating heart. I could feel it echo in my ears, sounding like a warm drum. He rested his chin on my head as his hands stretched across my back. They took up the entire area, feeling me everywhere.

I felt so small in his arms. He could break me in half if he wanted. But I also felt safe, like nothing could ever hurt me. He wouldn't let anything ever happen to me. He was one of the good guys—the best.

He pulled his face away slightly then looked down at me. His lips hovered just inches from my forehead, ready to lean in for a kiss.

I'd never been kissed that way before, and now I didn't know how I felt about it. It seemed so innocent, so safe. But my heart was about to burst out of my chest in fear.

"Can I kiss you?"

My heart skipped a beat. I tried to breathe but I couldn't. I felt light-headed from the rush of blood that entered my heart. It was overloaded and unable to keep up with the adrenaline.

"Please."

Unable to speak, I just nodded.

He cupped my face and pressed a kiss to my forehead. His lips felt hot against my skin, soft and wet. The kiss was slow and lingered indefinitely. It didn't seem like he would ever pull away—not until the end of time.

My heart fluttered at the touch, feeling a high that would never dissipate.

He pulled away and dropped his hands. "Good night, sweetheart."

"Good night…" I couldn't get over that kiss and the way it made me feel. My legs were weak and my eyes were heavy.

He gave me a final look before he walked away. His massive shoulders moved as he walked, and his hard back was rigid and straight. He was a powerhouse on two legs, formidable and inviting all at the same time.

I looked at the keys in my hand and felt the hot metal. My hands were so warm and sweaty that they heated up the metal until they were uncomfortably hot. They felt slippery in my grasp.

I didn't want to insert them into the door and walk inside. I didn't want to walk in there alone. For the past four years all I've ever craved is solitude. No one understood what I went through, and no man would ever trick me again. But now I didn't want to be alone. I wanted him to walk inside with me—and never leave.

CHAPTER SEVENTEEN

Kyle

Despite how tired I was, I kept going. I'd had eight cups of coffee, two Rock Stars, and a shot of espresso—all in a single day. This case was the most important thing to me at the moment, and I was giving my all. Actually, I was giving over a hundred percent.

My client was important to me. After all, she was the victim of this particular incident. But Rose was the person who truly fueled me forward. The more I spent time with her, the more I fell for her.

I had to make this right.

Mark tried to fight for the case a few times, insisting it should be his since he defended Rose the first time. No offense to him, but I didn't trust anyone else to get this done right. I needed to be the prosecutor in the courtroom. I needed to bring that asshole down.

The only bad thing about my devotion was my lack of time. I wanted to see Rose more often but I simply couldn't. When I wasn't working, I still needed to sleep and eat. They were necessities for life.

Our relationship was doing very well. She stopped pushing me away and making excuses not to see me anymore. She was finally comfortable around me, trusting me in a way she didn't trust anyone else.

It took us two months to get to this level, and I was relieved it finally happened.

I wanted something more with her, something physical. But I knew she wasn't ready for that. I was a patient man and I could wait as long as she wanted, but I hoped I wouldn't have to wait forever.

Even a kiss would satisfy me.

I knew Rose was broken and may never be the same after what happened to her. Any other guy would tell me to walk away. I was walking into a situation that would suffocate me. She would always be damaged, and she may not give me the kind of love I wanted.

But I wanted her.

For whatever reason, I was connected to her. She made me feel things no other woman ever could. When I wasn't with her, I thought about her nonstop. And even when I was standing right in front of her, I missed her.

I couldn't walk away.

No one ever made me as happy as she did. When she laughed at my jokes and smiled from across the table I melted inside. Maybe she was still a wreck at the moment, but I really believed I could fix her.

I could put her back together.

***

"Haven't seen you in forever."

I slid into the booth across from Will, a dark IPA in my hand. "You know, the law never sleeps."

"You took on a case?"

"Yeah, a pretty big one. The defendant has been charged with the crime before but he walked free. This time this fucker is walking to jail."

"If anyone can nail him, it's you."

And I would nail him.

"So, what's new with you?"

He didn't ask me about Rose, to my surprise. "Nothing really."

235

"Nothing?" he asked. "Then why haven't you called me?"

"Are you a girl now?" I snapped. "The phone works two ways."

"Whatever." He took a drink of his beer.

"I've been spending a lot of time with Rose..." I didn't want to hide what I was doing. I told him I was going to go for her, so I had nothing to hide anyway.

"Wait, what?" he asked. "You're dating her?"

"I've been dating her for a while." Why was that a surprise to him?

Now his beer was untouched, and he stared at me like he couldn't believe what I was saying. "You're serious?"

"Did you think I was joking last time I brought her up?" I asked incredulously. "I told you I was into her and I was going for it."

"But she said yes?"

"Why wouldn't she?" I kept the offense bottled deep inside.

"Florence made it sound like Rose had no intention of being with you."

She said that? Maybe she said it a long time ago. Things had only recently changed in the past few weeks. "In the beginning she was hesitant, but things are different now."

"Well, Florence doesn't know that…"

"Why does it matter?" The only people who mattered in our relationship were Rose and I.

"Florence was really into you…"

"Yes, I remember."

"Well, I don't think she's going to be happy when she finds out her best friend is seeing you."

I rolled my eyes dramatically. "Well, she'll get over it."

"I don't think she will."

"Why don't you two date?" I snapped. "You're both equally annoying."

"Whoa, calm down." He raised both hands in the air. "I'm just telling you the facts. I'm bummed it didn't work out with Rose and I, but I've made my peace with it. But Florence…it's different with her. She'll see this as a betrayal."

I didn't understand women sometimes. "She'd really stop her friend from being with me? It's not Rose's fault I preferred her to Florence. And Florence shouldn't take it so seriously. Not every date she goes on is going to end with a happily ever after. She needs to get over herself."

"Maybe. But that doesn't change anything."

Nothing was going to get between Rose and me. What she and I had was special. It was real and true. It wasn't exactly traditional, and sometimes it was a little complicated, but that didn't change anything. We were sticking together. "Whatever. I'll deal with it when the time comes."

"Wow. So you really like this girl."

I more than liked her. "Yes."

"Have you guys...?"

He asked me these questions before, about the other women I'd been with. His curiosity never bothered me—until now. "None of your business."

"Come on, don't get prissy about it."

"Then don't ask me about it."

"She's, like, one of the hottest—"

"Finish that sentence and I'll break your neck."

He shut his mouth, but his eyes burned with anger.

"Don't talk about my girl like that. Not if you want to live."

***

Wednesday came and went, but I didn't call her. Not because I didn't want to see her. I simply got lost in time and didn't even know what day of the week it was. The judge for the trial had been selected and they were already scheduling everything.

I had to take advantage of every single minute.

By Friday, I realized it'd been nearly a week since I'd seen her or even talked to her. With her, it wasn't a big deal because she preferred being alone anyway. Some space would keep her calm, keep our relationship as smooth as possible.

I was sitting at my kitchen table with a cup of coffee beside me. I was going over my notes and my dictations. Despite all the caffeine in my system I was exhausted. There was nothing I wanted more than to collapse on my bed and go to sleep.

A knock on my front door broke my concentration.

I wasn't expecting company, and I hoped it wasn't a booty call stopping by. I didn't do those anymore and I hated taking the time to explain that to my regulars. They usually got upset and caused a scene. And I had to stand there and wait until they were finished.

I opened the door and saw someone I'd never expected to see on my doorstep.

Rose.

Her hair was pulled back into a high ponytail, and the red sheen of her hair shined under the florescent lights. She wore a purple dress with sandals, and her makeup was done in a nice way. In her hands was a picnic basket.

I couldn't keep the surprise off my face. She was actually standing outside my apartment—willingly.

She looked up at me with hesitant eyes, like she regretted coming down there now that she was standing in front of me. It took a lot of courage to come all the way here, and now she was second-guessing it. "I'm sorry…I shouldn't be here. I didn't mean to bother you."

I took the picnic basket from her hand then wrapped my free arm around her waist. Without asking for permission or thinking twice about it, I pressed a kiss to her forehead.

She flinched at the touch but quickly melted a second later.

"I'm so glad to see you." I squeezed her side affectionately then grabbed her hand.

The uncertainty disappeared from her eyes.

I pulled her inside my apartment and placed the picnic basket on the table.

"I didn't mean to barge in. I just wanted to drop that off. Thought you might be hungry…"

There was no way she got dressed up like that just to drop off some food. "Eat with me."

A small smile stretched her lips even though she tried to hide it. "If I'm not interrupting anything."

"No, you aren't." I walked to the table and spotted the picture of her on the surface. Panic exploded in my brain and I quickly shuffled everything together and stashed it away. If she saw that picture, she'd figure out what I was working on.

And that was not the best way for her to find out.

I shoved everything inside my briefcase then shut it before I placed it under the table, out of sight and out of mind.

She set the picnic basket on the surface and opened the lid. "I made sandwiches and salads. Hope you're hungry."

"Starving." I pulled out the chair for her before I sat down. I was in the middle of dictating when she came to my door, but I quickly pushed the case to the back of my mind. When she was in my presence, she stole all my attention.

She sat down and passed the plastic containers to me. "Sorry, I didn't have anything cuter than that."

"It's perfect." I opened the lids and began to eat.

She kept her eyes on her food, like she was afraid to look at me. Her lack of confidence was returning, and she was uneasy all over again. "Since I hadn't heard from you in a while, I just wanted to stop by…"

Was she afraid that I was going to leave? That I lost interest and moved onto someone else? "Sorry. I got busy with my case and lost track of time. I think I've gotten twelve hours of sleep in the past week." That wasn't an exaggeration.

"Is it a complicated case? Do you have other lawyers working on it with you?"

"It's not necessarily complicated, but I want to make sure there's no chance of losing. And no, I'm doing this one solo."

"Can you have another lawyer if you wanted to?"

"Yeah. But I prefer to work alone."

She took a few bites of her salad, growing quiet.

"I'm glad you stopped by. I needed to take a break anyway."

"I'm glad I'm not bothering you."

"You can stop by whenever you want." I really meant that. She could come and go whenever she pleased. It didn't bother me in the least. I had nothing to hide and no one better to spend my time with.

"Yeah?" Her eyes turned back to me, searching my face.

"Absolutely." I ate the food she brought, thankful for a home-cooked meal. I'd been eating out a lot because I hadn't had time to do anything else. The sluggish aftershock of heavy meals was starting to get to me. That made her picnic taste even better.

She finished her food then carefully sealed the lids back on the plastic containers. "Well, I'll let you go. I just wanted to stop by and visit."

"You aren't going anywhere." I returned everything to the basket and closed it.

"I'm not?"

"No. Let's watch a movie or something."

"Are you sure? I don't want to keep you away from your work."

"Believe me, I need a break." I walked to the couch and took a seat at the very end. She usually sat in the opposite corner, keeping the middle seat between us. But this time, she sat directly next to me.

My heart was beating faster than it ever had before.

She came by my apartment just to see me, and now she was beside me. I wasn't sure what I was doing to make her this comfortable around me, but I needed to keep it up.

"What do you want to watch?"

"I'm not picky."

I turned on the TV and found Toy Story.

"I love Disney movies."

"Anyone who doesn't is a weirdo."

She crossed her legs, her toned thighs catching my attention, and she watched the movie with her hands in her lap.

Instead of watching the screen, I watched her. I wasn't allowed to stare at her in the past, but now it felt appropriate. I could look at her when I wanted and however long I wanted.

When she felt my gaze burn into her cheek, she turned my way.

E. L. Todd

I didn't pull my gaze away, refusing to avert my eyes. I loved staring at her features, studying the curve of her eyes as well as her lips. Her hair fell over one shoulder and I remembered how soft it felt in my fingers. Her curves and her sweet mouth made me hard in my jeans, but I wanted her for so many more reasons.

A million reasons.

Her breathing picked up the longer our eyes locked. Her fingers fidgeted in her lap as the stare continued. Instead of looking away like she usually did she kept staring.

"Does this make you uncomfortable?"

Her lips parted slightly, showing her small teeth. "No."

My arms scooped underneath her small frame, just as they would if I were going to pick her up.

Rose watched what I was doing, unsure what was going to happen next.

I moved to her to a laying position, having her lay down right beside me on the couch. My back was to the TV because I wasn't going to watch it anyway. I grabbed the blanket hanging off the back of the couch and pulled it over our bodies. This was the most affection we've ever

245

shared, but she seemed okay with it. My face was close to hers and I rested my arm around her waist, feeling the small indentions of her ribs. "Is this okay?"

Her voice cracked before she spoke. "Yes."

I naturally wanted to grab her thigh and wrap it around my waist, but since she was wearing a dress that might spook her. I kept her body exactly where it was and entertained myself by looking her in the eye.

Her almond shaped eyes were hypnotizing and bold. They were greener than the lushest lawn in summer, and they were softer than the pedals of a rose. She was delicate like a snowflake but hard as steel. I loved everything about her, from the tip of her nose to the curve of her lips. She was a work of art, absent of any flaws. She couldn't be any more perfect—for me.

Her breathing was still irregular, telling me she was nervous with our placement. It was the most affection we'd ever shared. We were laying together on the couch in an empty apartment. A kid's movie was on in the background, but neither one of us were paying attention to it.

I wanted to kiss her—badly.

But I knew she wasn't ready for that. She needed to come out of her shell a little more. If I went for the kiss the first time we were together like this, she might avoid intimacy altogether. She liked me because she felt safe with me. There was no pressure to do anything.

So I had to keep making her feel safe.

"How have you been?" My hand moved to her lower back, feeling the prominent curve there. It was one of the attributes I found most sexy on a woman, and it didn't surprise me that she had it. I wanted to run kisses along the area, moving down her ass to the sweet spot I desired most. The thought made me hard so I shook it away, not wanting her to feel the bulge in my jeans. Of all things, that would make her the most uncomfortable.

"Good. Just work and jogging."

"And eating ice cream?" I teased.

"No, I've stayed strong. I walk right past it with my head held high."

"You deserve a treat after running six miles."

"But then I'm eating back all the calories I burned. Seems counterproductive."

Like she needed to worry about calorie counting. "Anything else?"

"I got a new client. He wants me to build his office in Manhattan. It's a big project and I'm excited to start."

"Are you still working on mine?"

"Honestly, no. I guess I'm trying to drag it out as long as possible..." Her hand slowly moved across the couch until it rested in the center of my chest. Her fingers lightly rubbed the area, her eyes glued to her actions.

"You know I'll still be here if and when you finish the project." And I'd here long after that. Feeling her touch me like that sent shivers down my spine. It was the most affection I got from her, and it was sexy. It felt like more than just an innocent touch, that she was attracted to my size and build.

She wanted me.

"Yeah?" she whispered.

I nodded.

I wanted to kiss her so much it hurt. If it were any other woman I'd go for it, but I couldn't afford to make a mistake with Rose. Her desires had to be unmistakably clear.

My fingers felt the fabric of her dress along her back, feeling the softness of the fabric. The scent of her perfume washed over me, light and fragrant. Sometimes I wasn't sure if it was

E. L. Todd

perfume she sprayed on her wrists, or her natural scent altogether. Hopefully, I'd find that answer one day.

As the minutes trickled by, she realized nothing more would come from our interaction. Her lips were safe at the moment, and that made the rest of her body relax. Her fingers moved softly over my chest and down to my stomach, feeling the grooves from my abs. Her eyes took in my entire body, particularly the features of my face. She was exploring me, going at a pace suitable to her.

I couldn't even begin to understand what she went through. As a man, the thought of someone doing something to me against my will never crossed my mind. I walked the streets at night, never afraid someone would take my virtue. Maybe they'll take my wallet, but that would be the worst of it. After what she went through it didn't surprise me how closed off she was. Could she ever feel turned on again? When that was her last experience?

Maybe this was all she could handle.

"Kyle?" When she said my mine it sounded too sexy to ignore. She had a naturally beautiful voice, and it was hypnotizing and achingly warm.

"Sweetheart?" I usually called girls baby, but a different nickname emerged for Rose.

"Why haven't you kissed me? Why haven't you tried anything?"

The question surprised me. I couldn't think of a single reason why she asked it. "It doesn't seem like you want me to."

"But how do you know that?" Her hand rested on my chest, directly over my heart.

"I just do." My hand slid further up her back, feeling her body expand with every breath she took.

"That doesn't bother you...?"

"Why would it?" My hand reached her long strands of brown hair, and I fingered it slightly.

"I don't know...I'm not fast like the women you're used to."

She must be comparing herself to Cassandra, who would take me then and there if I asked her to. "I don't want you to be fast. I want you to be you."

"But it must disappoint you." She searched my eyes for a lie.

"It doesn't. I don't expect anything, and I'll gladly take anything you give me."

Her eyes moved to my chest. "I don't know what this is, Kyle. I wanted to stay away from you but I couldn't. Now here I am...unable to get away."

"Isn't that a good thing?"

"I'm not right for you. I can't do relationships, and I can't do commitments. I'm afraid I'm wasting your time."

"You're the only woman I want to be with. So you can never waste my time." I wish she would just tell me what happened four years ago. I wish she would trust me to see her in the exact same light. What happened to her was a crime, but she didn't need to be ashamed of it. "I like things the way they are and I don't want them to change. So don't think about where this may go or what's in the past. Let's just live in the moment—together." I pulled her closer to me so our bodies were touching. I wanted to feel her chest press against mine every time she took a breath. I wanted to hear the quiet sighs that escaped her lips because I was close enough to catch them. I wanted more than this, everything she could possibly give me. But I'd settle for much less—because she was special.

Saturday

CHAPTER EIGHTEEN

Rose

Without realizing it, I'd fallen for Kyle.

When we weren't together, I missed him. When he didn't call me, I hoped he was just busy. When he held me on the couch and didn't pressure me do anything, even kiss him, I felt indebted to him.

I'd never met a man like him.

Most men wanted to get laid on the first date. They were sweet and charming, but a physical relationship was essential for their needs. They pressured me into things I wasn't ready for, and since it reminded me so much of that night I stopped trying altogether.

Then I met Kyle.

He was content holding my hand and nothing else. He didn't make a move on me even when he had the right to. Two months had come and gone, and he still didn't kiss me.

Who had that kind of willpower?

He seemed too good to be true.

He was sensitive, caring, and he made me laugh. Which was a surprise because no one ever made me laugh. He was drop-dead gorgeous, having the looks of a model and the body of a soldier.

And he was interested in me.

How did that I get that lucky?

Sometimes I thought I could forget about the past and move on—with Kyle. If we took things slow we might be able to have the kind of sex I could enjoy. I may be able to push out all the memories of that terrible night and actually enjoy it.

Sex was something I loved once upon a time. I'd had long-term relationships and a few flings, and hitting the sheets was always fantastic. I enjoyed it just as much as men did.

But now I was drier than a desert.

My body hadn't woken up from the drought in four years. Nothing excited me anymore, and when I did think about sex I remembered what happened to me. It was a vicious cycle, so I put sex out of my mind for good. I didn't even masturbate.

But with Kyle, I felt my body come to life.

Sometimes I fantasized about kissing him, feeling those thin lips against mine. Sometimes I wondered what he looked like shirtless, all muscle. Sometimes I wondered how his naked body would feel against mine. The vision lasted for a few minutes, beautiful and arousing. My body responded in a way it never did when I thought about sex. I became wet and turned on.

But is that how I would feel in real life?

If we became physical would I get scared and run?

Was it worth the chance?

Maybe I should just tell him what happened. He seemed caring and understanding. And he would finally know why I was so prude. He was dealing with a woman who experienced a serious trauma. He was basically walking into a mine field in the dark.

But I was scared.

He wouldn't want me anymore.

He would think about the things that happened and become disgusted.

He'd never look at me the same.

Saturday

Wasn't it better just to keep it a secret? How would he ever find out anyway?

Or would that be deceitful?

Ugh, I couldn't make up my mind.

Someone pounded on my door, shattering the internal debate I was having. "Rose, it's me. Open the door." Florence pounded on the wood again.

What was she doing here? I left the table where my sketching supplies were and opened the door. "Is everything okay?" She hardly dropped by my apartment. She usually texted me first.

"I talked to Will today."

Who was Will again?

She walked inside without being invited. "He said Kyle told him you two were dating." She crossed her arms over her chest and gave me the coldest look I've ever seen. "Is that true?"

Kyle thought we were dating? To me, we were just friends that spent time together. But when I reflected on the things we did together, cuddling on the couch and holding each other at the end of the night I realized that wasn't true. "Yes."

Now her eyes burned with fire. "What the hell, Rose? You told me you weren't into him."

"I said I would never date him."

"Isn't that the same damn thing? He was my guy. How could you take him away from me?"

Her cattiness and stubbornness never bothered me because it wasn't directed at me. It was always aimed at the people outside our inner circle. But now that it was my problem, I didn't like it. "I didn't take him away from you, Florence. We just had a connection and we got tired of fighting it."

"But you knew how much I liked him. How could you do that as my friend?"

I kept my voice calm so she would stop screaming. "You only went out twice."

"What does that matter? We kissed and I thought it would go somewhere."

"But it's not like he was your boyfriend and you broke up. I think you're being unfair."

"No, I'm not. You broke the girl code."

"Look, I didn't date him right off the bat. He kept pursuing me and he wouldn't give up. This went on for weeks before I finally caved. When I got to know him better, I ended up really liking him. I'm sorry that I hurt your feelings, Florence. I never meant to do that."

"Does that mean you're going to stop seeing him?"

She couldn't be serious. "What would that solve?"

"How are we supposed to hang out and be friends when there's an elephant in the room?"

By getting over it. "If I stop seeing him, he's not going to see you."

"But it's still a strain on our relationship. What's more important? A boyfriend or a friend?" She shifted her weight to one leg and venomously glared at me.

"Why does there have to be a decision at all? Florence, this is the first time I've ever been with a guy that I've actually liked. I don't think about what happened when I'm with him. I think I can finally move on. Isn't that the most important thing here?"

"I still think it's a conflict of interest. You knew how much I was into him."

"I do," I admitted. "But he makes me happy. We're happy together." I didn't think I could give him up. I'd grown so attached to him, attached to the way he made me feel.

"Fine. Then you've made your decision." She backed up, angry tears in her eyes.

"That's it?" I asked incredulously. "I have to dump him or you won't be my friend anymore?"

"We both know he was mine first." She marched out the door and slammed it hard behind her.

Speechless, I just stood there. The last thing she said kept playing in my mind. I could hardly believe what she said. "No. He was always mine."

***

For the next few days all I could think about was Florence. Her reaction was childish and irritating, but I couldn't help but feel terrible for what I did to her. The guilt was eating me alive.

After that terrible night four years ago, she was there for me. She was by my side every second of the day, getting me back on my feet. And as the years passed, she didn't let my troubles drown me. She forced me to go out with her, to meet new people. She basically took my hand and guided me to recovery.

So could I really do this to her?

She didn't know Kyle the way I did. She didn't have the same kind of connection with him. But she did feel something for him, enough to throw a tantrum. While I liked Kyle and the way he made me feel, we had no future together. Once I told him what happened, he would be too uncomfortable to stick around—and I wouldn't blame him. And even if he was okay with it, would I ever be able to make love to him? Would sex always get in the way? I knew he was a promiscuous man just from looking at Cassandra.

We were doomed to fail regardless.

Even if we were about to go our separate ways, Kyle gave me hope. He was a good man that wouldn't hurt a fly. If he existed, then there must be others. Not everyone was sinister with sinister intentions.

But that didn't make this any easier.

***

I stopped by his apartment one evening after work. I didn't call him ahead of time. If I did, he would hear the sadness in my voice and know something was wrong. It was easier to walk inside and drop the bomb quickly—get it over with.

He opened the door with a smile on his face, happy to see me. He wore a gray t-shirt with running shorts, what he usually wore around the house. His arms were toned and muscular, and his calves were thick and powerful. Kyle was unnaturally good looking. Sometimes I wondered if he was my imaginary friend. "Hey."

His arm hooked around my waist and he pulled me into his chest for a hug.

"Hey."

Like always, his mouth moved to my forehead. "I missed you."

I melted into a puddle at his feet, victim to his words and his kiss. "I missed you too."

He shut the door then wrapped his other arm around me, enveloping me tighter than a letter. His arms were as solid as metal bars, and nothing could get to me when I was inside. "I was just thinking about you."

"You were?"

"Yeah. But then again, I'm always thinking about you." He slowly pulled his arms away, reluctant to let me go. "Would you like anything? Something to drink?"

His question returned me to the present. I was there for a reason, and if I let his sweet words and warm touch affect me, I'd never leave. Kyle had the unnatural ability to make me fall headfirst.

Along with every other woman in the world.

"No, thank you. Actually...I need to talk to you about something."

He stiffened in front of me, his eyes changing. One moment he was looking at me with fondness, and now he was staring at me with fear. He scanned my face, searching for the words I hadn't spoken. "No."

His response didn't make sense, so I had no idea what he meant. "What?"

"No. You aren't leaving."

How'd he know...?

He gripped both of my wrists and placed them over his chest. "I'm not letting you go, Rose. When you get scared, talk to me. But don't leave."

Did I make it that obvious? Or could he read me that well?

"I'll do anything to make this work," he whispered. "Whatever you need, it's yours. You just have to tell me."

"Kyle, it's not you."

"Then I'll fix whatever it is."

"It's not something you can fix."

He brought one hand to his lips and kissed the skin over my knuckles. "Talk to me."

"It's Florence. She found out we were seeing each other and she wasn't happy about it."

"How's that our problem?"

"Because she's my friend."

"What does that matter? She should be happy for you."

"Well, she doesn't see it that way," I whispered. "She dated you first and really liked you. It hurts her feelings that I'm dating a man that she really wanted—that she called dibs on."

His eyes immediately darkened. "The second you walked into that restaurant, I was yours. And you know that."

I tried to ignore the sweet thing he just said. "She said it's a conflict of interest and she's never going to be okay with it."

"That's not our problem. Don't let her manipulate you. We're happy together and she's the one being selfish."

"You don't understand…"

"Actually, I do," he said coldly. "What kind of friend tells you to break up with a guy that you really like? I'm the first guy you've been with in forever, and she wants you to—"

"Wait…how did you know that?"

"Know what?" He kept a straight face.

"That you're the only guy I've been with in a long time."

He stared at the ground before he looked at me again. "The same way I knew something was wrong once you walked in the door. I can't explain it, Rose. I just know. And I think Florence is a really shitty friend."

"But she was there for me…in the past. She did a lot for me when I didn't ask her to."

"Even so, you don't owe her anything. She's just jealous that I like you instead of her."

"You didn't see her face. She started to cry—"

"Then she needs to grow up," he snapped. "Even if you broke up with me, I'm not going to date her. So she doesn't get what she wants either way. She may as well let us be."

He had the same arguments I did, but it didn't change Florence's mind. "Boyfriends come and go but friends are forever. I can't pick a guy over her."

He stared me down, his blue eyes no longer as brilliant. He glanced at my lips before he looked me head-on again. "I'm not going to come and go, Rose. Surely, you must know that by now."

I forgot to breathe.

"I've never felt this way for anyone before, not even Francesca. And I was going to marry her. Whatever we have is different than anything else we've ever experienced. I realize we've only known each other for three months, and I sound crazy right now, but I know this is going to last. I'm not just some guy. I'm the guy."

I finally took a breath, feeling my lungs ached from being deprived of oxygen for so long. What he said was both beautiful and terrifying. Unsure what to say back, I just stood there.

"I realize how that must sound. But I know you understand exactly what I'm talking about. I'm not crazy, and neither are you."

There were times when I knew what he was referring to, especially the first time we met. Simple touches felt explosive and hot. I trusted him when I didn't think I could trust anyone as long as I lived. So much had happened in such a short amount of time. It was unbelievable.

"No," Kyle said. "We aren't going our separate ways. End of story."

Despite the truth of everything he said, there was still other problems on the horizon. He didn't know the truth of what happened to me. And if he did it would change everything. He wouldn't be fighting for me so hard. He wouldn't look at me like that anymore, like I was the only person who mattered in the world. But selfishly, I didn't say a word.

Saturday

CHAPTER NINETEEN

Kyle

Rose and I already had obstacles coming our way, and I couldn't afford any unnecessary hurdles.

Florence was an unnecessary hurdle.

Her jealousy wasn't going to come between us, and I certainly wasn't going to let her make Rose feel guilty for being with me. Or worse, manipulate her into breaking up with me.

What the hell was Will thinking when he first set me up with her?

Rose could defend her and claim Florence was there for her when she needed her most, probably after the trauma happened, but I knew friends wanted their friends to be happy—not break up with the man they cared most about.

If we didn't have the strong connection we felt every day, it might be easier just to throw in the towel and walk away. But I wasn't walking away from Rose—not now and not ever.

I approached Florence's door and knocked. I came here in the hope of fixing this situation so Rose could do whatever the hell she wanted. If I patched things up, then Rose could move on guilt-free. If I didn't take care of this now, it would only haunt us later.

Florence opened the door looking pissed—as usual. "What do you want?"

I ignored her rudeness. "If you're free, I'd love to take you out for a drink."

She crossed her arms over her chest. "You're asking me out?"

Did she assume that every time someone wanted to spend time with her? She reeked of desperation, and that was such a turn off. "No. I wanted to talk about something."

"Rose?"

"Yes." What else could I possibly want to talk about?

"Oh..."

Apparently, we were going to have this conversation right outside her door. "I understand how you feel about Rose and I. Honestly, I get it."

She listened, her attitude still at an all-time high.

If I were going to get her on board I'd have to play on her enormous ego. Confidence was sexy in a woman, but arrogance was a boner killer. And she was definitely arrogant. "We both know you're out of my league. It never would have worked between us. Somewhere down the road, you would have found someone better and I couldn't handle that kind of rejection."

Her eyes immediately softened, clearly not expecting those words to come out of my mouth.

"Rose and I are more compatible. We both have issues, similar ones. Maybe she's not as good as you, but I think we can really have something based on friendship. I know she's been through a lot and so have I." Acid emerged from the back of my throat, but I ignored it. I didn't believe anything I was saying, but I was willing to do anything to get her off Rose's back—even if I had to lie.

"So, you want me, but you don't think you're good enough for me?"

Whatever you want to hear. "Exactly. You're meant for Prince Charming. Me? I'm some lawyer who's losing his firm."

"You're losing your firm?" she asked in surprise.

"Yeah...business has been terrible so I'm going bankrupt. I'll have to sell my beach house and everything." I pouted my lips and tried to look as desolated as possible.

"That's terrible..."

"Yeah. My credit is terrible too. I'll never be able to get another loan." She only wanted me for my looks and my money, so if I made myself look as undesirable as possible she'd probably lose interest. In fact, she'd probably be grateful it didn't work out.

"I'm so sorry..."

"Well, what are you going to do?" I said with a shrug. "Rose will probably support me."

She cringed.

"So, if you really think about it, you dodged a bullet."

"Yeah...I'll say."

Now I wish I'd said this crap a long time ago. "One minute you're at the top, and the next minute you're at the bottom."

She took an involuntary step back, disgusted.

"So, I hope you can get on board with this. I'd really like it if we were friends."

"Yeah, sure." She prepared to close the door like she couldn't get away from me quick enough. "Rose is probably a better fit anyway."

Much better.

"Yeah, she's pretty great. I think we go well together."

She shut the door.

The conversation was finally over and I took a deep breath. Then I smiled.

**

Rose opened the door, surprised to see me stop by. "Hey."

"Hey." I stepped inside without being invited, finally getting to a comfortable point in our relationship when I could do that sort of thing.

Rose was closed off all over again, probably because the issue with Florence was still bothering her. "What's up?"

"I just talked to Florence."

"You did?" She stiffened in surprise.

"Yeah, I fixed everything with her so we're good."

"What do you mean you fixed everything?" she asked.

"I played to her ego a little bit." Okay, a lot. "I told her she was way out of my league and I was settling for you..."

Rose tried not to laugh.

"And if she asks, my business is going under and I don't have a job."

"What?" she said with a laugh. "Are you serious?"

"I knew she was only into me for my looks and money, so when I told her I was losing my beach house, she looked at me like scum. She couldn't get away from me fast enough."

"Oh my god." She covered her mouth and chuckled to herself.

"Whatever. It worked."

"I can't believe you did that."

"I had to get her off your back. She shouldn't make you feel guilty for being happy. That's not what real friends do." I was surprised Rose continued to stand by Florence when she was so exhausting. But she must have really done something to deserve it.

"I can't believe you threw yourself under the bus."

"I don't care. Better me than you."

She smiled at me, the look reaching her beautiful green eyes. "Well, thank you for doing that."

"I'd do anything for you." In a heartbeat.

Her cheeks slightly reddened and her gaze shifted to my chest. Whenever I was particularly sweet to her, she blushed.

"The Warrior game is on right now. Want to watch it?"

"Yeah, I'd love to."

I put my arm around her waist and walked with her to the couch. "I got here at the perfect time."

***

The trial had been scheduled. It was exactly two weeks from today.

A part of me was nervous. But the bigger part of me couldn't wait to get started. My arsenal was packed with ammo, and I was eager to rip that guy to pieces. I wouldn't settle for anything less than life in prison, and since this was his second offense there was a good chance I would get it.

Mark walked into my office. "I heard the good news."

Saturday

"What good news?" I just finished emailing the district attorney. We were supposed to golf together on Saturday.

"That the trial is scheduled. Sometimes these things take forever to take off. Good thing they were quick on this one."

"Yeah." I was prepared for that trial. I didn't stop until I had every little detail ironed out. I was going to wipe the floors clean with his dead body.

"You're sure you don't need any help?" He approached my desk with his hands in his pockets. "Two minds are better than one, right?"

"Thanks, Mark. But I've got this."

"Is Rose Perkins going to testify?"

I tried not to react to her name. "No."

"Really?" he asked. "I assumed she'd want to."

"Since her case was dismissed, I don't think her testimony will have any real impact."

"It doesn't hurt to try."

"No, I'm keeping her out of this. She already suffered through it once. No need for her to go through it again."

He paused in front of my desk, his eyes glued to my face. "You're telling me she doesn't know?"

274

I wasn't purposely keeping it from her. She could find out in many other ways. But I didn't think it would do her any good if she knew. It would bring back a lot of painful memories, and if I lost the case it would just make her feel worse. After I won the case, I'd tell her the truth. "No."

"Don't you think she has the right to know? Her assaulter is on trial again?"

"You really want to put that sweet girl through that again?" I asked coldly.

Mark gave me a new look, full of suspicion. "Do you know Rose or something?"

"Not personally." I lied through my teeth, not wanting to make this a conflict of interest.

"Because you're behaving oddly. I've never seen you handle a case like this."

The third degree was starting to burn me. "Mark, I've been practicing law for a long time now, and I worked in this office all through my education. I learned from the best in the business, and I'm not in it for the money. I do this job every day to help people. Right now, I'm trying to help Rose and Audrey. Maybe if you got off my ass I'd be able to do that."

**

Mom was in the city so she asked me to have dinner with her. She was probably shopping downtown, and she would have invited me if shopping were a hobby of mine. My sister used to do that sort of thing with her all the time. Even all these years later, her absence was still noticed.

Rose texted me as I was getting ready. Want to come over for dinner tonight?

There was nothing I wanted more. I'd love to. But I already have dinner plans with my mom.

Oh. That's too bad.

But I can come over afterward. For dessert. By the time I realized how that message sounded, it was too late. I already sent it. Shit. I mean, we can hang out afterward. Watch a movie or something. The paranoia was settling and I was afraid I really screwed this up.

Yeah, that sounds good.

Thank god. That could have gone over much differently. Alright, I'll see you then.

K.

I stared at the phone and typed another message. Come to dinner with me.

With your mom?

Yeah, why not? I hoped she planned on meeting her anyway.

I don't think that's a good idea.

Why not?

It's short notice and I'm just not ready.

Fair enough. I was disappointed, but if I pushed her too hard I might make things worse. I'll see you when we're finished.

Okay.

***

We chatted quietly over dinner, making small talk about work and the case I was working on. She told me she was going to a charity event next weekend, and she needed a new pair of shoes for her dress.

"So...anyone special in your life?" This question always came up—every single time. "Anything happen with that girl who stayed at your place?" All she wanted was for me to settle down and be happy. After Francesca left me she thought I was a wounded dog that would never get better.

"Actually, yeah."

"Yeah what?" She dropped her fork onto her plate, making a loud clanking sound.

"I'm seeing someone—that girl from the beach house."

"That's wonderful." Her voice went up a few octaves. "Absolutely wonderful. Why didn't you bring her along?"

"I wanted it just to be us."

"Tell me everything about her."

I appreciated my mom's enthusiasm, but she took it too far sometimes. "She's an architect in the city. She's a brunette with green eyes, and she has the soul of a nun. She's beautiful, to say the least. And I really like her."

"Awe, that's so wonderful."

"But whether I have a girlfriend or not, I'm okay."

Mom looked away, guilty.

"Francesca and I have been broken up for a long time and I'm in a good place—so is she. I'm happy for her. You don't need to worry about me."

"She's a two-timing little bitch, if you ask me."

"Mom." I didn't owe Francesca anything, but I still cared about her. She was always faithful to me, but her heart couldn't deny what it wanted. She should have been with Hawke to begin with—and I should have bowed out the second time. "Don't talk about her like that."

"What?" she said innocently. "It's the truth."

"She made the right choice." Not just because she was clearly destined for Hawke, but because I knew she wasn't the right person for me. When Rose walked into my life everything

278

became clear. I was grateful things didn't work out with Francesca—because I never would have been as happy.

Mom picked at her food, the hostility still hovering around her.

"Anyway, I really like her."

"What's her name?"

"Rose."

"Oh my god, Kyle." She clutched her heart. "That's such a beautiful name."

"I know." It suited her perfectly.

"So, do you *like* like her? Or do you like love her?"

I rolled my eyes. "Mom…"

"Please tell me. What kind of relationship is this?"

Since I never had serious relationships, I thought being in one would be enough. "It's going somewhere."

"You just made your mother very happy. I need grandchildren before I die."

"You'll get them, Mom. I promise."

"Thank you, Kyle."

I poured another glass of wine because I needed it to get through this evening. All this talk of marriage and babies was disconcerting.

"So, there's something I want to talk to you about."

Oh no.

"Charles and I have set a date."

"Oh, that's great." This was a topic I could deal with.

"We're getting married in two weeks."

That was rushed. "You can get everything together in that timeframe?"

"It's going to be small, maybe ten people there."

That was something I could get on board with. "Where?"

"Cannes, France."

An international wedding? "Oh..."

"It's so beautiful this time of year. I think it'll be perfect."

Whatever she wanted, I would be there for her.

"I was hoping you would give me away."

She didn't even need to ask. "Of course, Mom."

"Thank you, dear. You've been such a sweetheart through all of this. I know it can't be easy for you."

"Actually, it is easy. I want you to be happy."

"Awe…"

I suddenly realized the date. "Wait, two weeks from now?"

"Yes. Why? Did you have plans?"

"Not exactly…I have court."

"But that must be on a Monday, right?"

"We're picking the jury the Friday before."

"Oh…I guess we could move it, but I don't think we can."

I could hand the case over to Mark, but I refused to do that. With the flight being twelve hours, I'd be cutting it short flying there and then straight back. If I gave a good enough reason, I could reschedule the case. "I think I can work something out."

"Dear, don't worry about it. I know your work is important to you."

"It's okay, Mom. I'm not missing your wedding."

She gave me an affectionate smile.

"I'll figure something out."

"Please bring Rose with you. There's nothing that would make me happier than seeing you dance at my wedding—with someone special."

Somehow, she made her wedding about me again. "I'll ask."

Saturday

***

When I walked inside, I spotted the cupcakes on the table. Each one was decorated with a different colored flower with beads of frosting around it. It looked like something you'd get at The Muffin Girl.

"Dessert is served." Rose slid the cupcake onto a napkin and handed it over.

"Did you make these?" I asked in surprise.

"Yep. It took me all day, but it was worth it."

I took a bite, my eyes on her the entire time. "They're good. I didn't realize baking was a hobby of yours."

"It's not. But I needed a break from the design I was working on. Plus, you said you wanted something sweet."

I was glad she didn't take my comment the wrong way. "Thanks for making them. I might have to take some home."

"You can take them all. Otherwise, I'll just eat them."

I finished the cupcake and tossed the wrapper in the garbage. "I have to say, that's the best cupcake I've ever had."

"Really?" she asked in excitement. "I made them from scratch and I wasn't sure how they would turn out."

"They turned out delicious." I sat on the couch and watched her sit beside me.

"How was dinner with your mom?"

"Good. But she talks a lot."

She laughed. "Don't they all?"

"Well, she does especially."

Rose smiled. "You tease her, but I know you're fond of her."

"Very. She's my mom. She raised me."

"She raised you into a very fine, young man." She wrapped her arm through mine.

I loved when she touched me. "She's getting married in two weeks."

"That's great," she said. "Weddings are so much fun."

"And she's getting married in France."

"Wow. Talk about fancy."

"She said it's going to be small, with just a few people."

"Then why get married in France?"

I shrugged. "I don't know. It's her wedding."

"Well, I'm sure it'll be beautiful."

Saturday

I hoped she would come with me. But the fact we'd have to travel together and possibly stay in the same room together might deter her. We'd made a lot of progress, but I doubt she was ready for that. "I'd really love if you would come with me. But I completely understand if you're uncomfortable."

"You want me to come with you...?" Her mouth was slightly open in surprise.

"Of course." There's no one else I'd rather have by my side. "All the expenses are paid for, so don't worry about that."

"How long would we be gone for?"

"Probably the weekend."

She stared at the TV, her thoughts working behind her eyes.

"You don't have to answer me right now. We have some time."

"Are you sure it's good idea if I'm there? With your family?"

"My mom was the one who told me to invite you," I said with a chuckle.

"Really? You told her about me?"

"Yeah. Why wouldn't I? You're my girlfriend." It was a bold thing to say, but I didn't want to keep mislabeling us. We weren't friends anymore. What we had was more intimate than that.

To my relief, she looked happy. A smile was on her lips, and that joy reached her eyes. She didn't give me her answer, but I suspected her answer would probably be yes.

***

By the end of the night, she'd fallen asleep. Her head rested on my shoulder and she was out for the night. Anytime we watched TV together, she usually passed out before midnight.

I didn't mind because she looked cute when she was asleep.

Like always, I picked her up and carried her into her bedroom. Her shoes were already gone so I didn't have to worry about those. I tucked her into the bed and pulled the sheets over her, making sure she was comfortable before I walked back out into the living room.

Her couch was the most uncomfortable piece of furniture I'd ever slept on, but I'd tough it out. We usually spent the following day together when I spent the night, so it was an even trade.

I turned off the TV and grabbed the blanket hanging off the back of the couch. I was too tall to sleep comfortably, but the cushions were still better than the hardwood floor. When I adjusted myself I closed my eyes and tried to go to sleep.

A moment later, the sound of small feet hit the floorboards. The sound became louder as it drew near.

I opened my eyes and turned to the hallway, and standing there was Rose. She'd changed out of her clothes into her pajamas. The bottoms were plaid and loose, and her top was a plain white t-shirt.

I didn't know what she wanted so I just stared at her.

"Come to bed."

Did I really hear that? Or did I just dream it?

"That couch is way too small for you."

"I'm really okay." I didn't want an invitation out of pity.

She placed her hands together in front of her waist, most of her features covered in shadow. Only the lights from the city gave visibility. "But I want you to sleep with me."

That was as direct as she was going to get. And it was exactly what I needed to hear.

I left the couch and slowly walked to her, finding her pajamas arousing. They covered every inch of skin but the fact she wore them to bed made them look sexy. All I'd ever seen her in was regular clothes.

She turned around and walked into the bedroom, all the lights still off.

I knew this was just an invitation to sleep—and to cuddle. But that was it. It was more than she ever gave me before so I was grateful. I didn't want to wear jeans to bed, but I didn't dare take them off.

She got into bed and pulled the covers off. "You can take off your clothes if you want…"

I hesitated at the edge of the bed, unsure if I should do it or not. She wouldn't have given me the option if she weren't comfortable with it. I pulled off my shirt first, going for the less controversial piece of clothing. I tossed it on the ground at the bedside and watched her reaction.

Her eyes were wide and she stared at me without blinking. Her eyes were on my chest and she didn't move, frozen in place. She eyed my chest and shoulders, and I was pretty sure she swallowed the lump in her throat. Instead of looking uncomfortable and flustered, she looked mesmerized.

Since she was okay with that, I removed my jeans and stood in my boxers. I wasn't hard at the moment, which was a blessing because she was bound to notice it. And that might make her uncomfortable.

This time she looked away, as if she realized she was staring too much.

I wish she would stare more.

I pulled the covers back then slipped into bed beside her. The softness of the mattress immediately relaxed my tight back, and the smell of her washed over me immediately afterward. I lay on my back beside her, not making any kind of move toward her. If she wanted to touch me, she would go for it.

She turned on her side and faced me, her eyes no longer lidded with sleep. She stared at my chest and my stomach, her eyes stopping where the sheets covered my waist.

I wondered what she was thinking, if she wanted me to envelope her in my arms.

She slowly moved across the bed, adjusting the sheets so she could get through, and then she snuggled into my side. Her arm wrapped around my waist and her face was buried in my neck.

Feeling her touch my bare skin gave me a serious rush. The most skin contact we had was our hands. But now her naked palm was on my chest, feeling the slab of muscle. I felt my body increase a few degrees from the contact.

Feeling brave, I snaked my arm underneath her and wrapped it around her waist. She didn't object to the touch. In fact, it seemed like she loved it. She was lighter than a feather so I shifted her directly on top of me, wanting to lay across me all night long. I did my best not to think of sexual things, or the mere fact I was alone in a bed with her. In this position, there was no way she would miss my hard-on.

One hand rested on the small of her back while the other dug into her hair. She was the perfect size and weight to rest on top of me. It felt like a soft pillow keeping me warm.

When women spent the night, sometimes there was cuddling. But for the most part there wasn't. She stuck to her side of the bed and I stuck to mine. After the sex was finished, we were both hot and sweaty anyway.

But now all I wanted to do was cuddle with Rose.

I'd never gone to bed with a woman without actually sleeping with her. And if I did, we at least fooled around. But tonight was going to be rated G. And I was perfectly fine with that.

"I feel like I'm lying on the sidewalk..."

My hand gently caressed her back. "Sorry?"

"Because you're hard like cement."

"Oh…" I chuckled. "Thanks, I think."

"I've never been so comfortable in my life." Her hand migrated to my shoulder gently, where she rubbed the area lovingly.

I pulled the strands of hair off her face and pressed a kiss to her forehead, the only place I'd been allowed. It wasn't her lips, that sweet area I longed for, but it was still a part of her.

And I was grateful.

There was a possibility I was taking on something I couldn't handle. Rose never talked about what happened to her on that terrible night, so I had no way of understanding the depth of her pain. But if she was sleeping in the same bed with me that very moment, it was safe to say we made a lot of progress. "I'm comfortable too. You're like a stuffed animal—but better."

"I hope I'm not old and smelly…"

"A little," I said with a chuckle. "But I like it."

"I was so tired a moment ago and now I'm restless."

What did that mean? Was I getting my hopes up for no reason? "Want me to sing to you?"

"You can sing?" she asked in surprise.

"I'm all right. Not bad, but not Whitney Houston either."

"I'd love to hear you sing."

I kept my voice low, whispering under my breath. I sang an old lullaby my mom used to sing to my sister and me. It had short verses and a simple chorus. It was the first thing that came to mind.

Instead of falling asleep, her breathing had increased. Her fingers dug into me in excitement.

I closed my eyes and waited for her to say something.

"Could you sing it again...?"

"You want me to?"

"It was the most beautiful thing I've ever heard. Yes, I want you to sing it again."

"Whatever my sweetheart wants."

***

I got to the courtroom and took a seat, a pitcher of water placed in front of me along with a single glass. My client, Audrey, wasn't scheduled to make an appearance. Her presence wasn't necessary today, and I wasn't going to make her stand in this room for a second longer than she had to.

The defense walked inside, two of the best lawyers in Manhattan. They were from Howard and Stern, a respectable firm just a few blocks from mine. When it came down to it, this case was all business. But I was irritated the defendant could afford such expensive legal help. That's probably how he got off the first time.

But he wouldn't get off the second time.

Dressed in an orange jumpsuit with his hands in cuffs, Peter was escorted to the table on the opposite side of the aisle. He had thick black hair, and his beard was coming in from not shaving. I'd been calm every single day leading up to the trial, but now that I had to look at him in real life I was anything but calm.

I wanted to beat him to death with my chair.

This man took something that didn't belong to him, and he hurt the woman I cared most about. He was a pathetic excuse for a human being, and if I could kill him and get away with it, I would.

I'm not kidding.

I forced my gaze straight ahead because I couldn't bare the sight any longer. My hands were shaking and my head was becoming congested with rage. Despite my passion for the law I didn't respect the justice system.

It failed Rose.

The proceeding began and I made my case. "I'd like to reschedule the trial to a later date."

The judge seemed bored, like all the others I've dealt with. "Your reason?"

"My mother is getting married overseas. I only need to postpone the trial for a few days."

He considered my request silently, grinding his teeth together as he deliberated.

I tried not to stare at Peter and imagine breaking his skull.

After a minute of silence, the judge pronounced his decision. "We'll reschedule. But this is the only postponement you'll receive."

"Thank you, your honor." Judge Bates and I were on good terms. I served my internship directly under his wing, and he was a good friend to my father. I suspected his bias would come in handy for the trial.

At least luck was on my side.

"We'll reconvene the following week." Judge Bates struck his mallet down. "We'll let the jury know."

When I turned to leave, I got another look at Peter. His face was blank, without an ounce of emotion whatsoever. He looked like a serial killer, someone who was unable to feel a single ounce of remorse.

Moments like this made me wish we had the death penalty.

***

Since I had a long lunch that day, I decided to stop by Rose's office. Now that our relationship reached a new level, I could come and go whenever I wanted. I didn't need to make up a reason to see her.

I walked inside and saw her working at her desk. A mechanical pencil was in her hand and her eyes were glued hard to her paper. A calculator and a protractor sat beside her. She was so absorbed in her work she didn't even notice me walk inside.

"Hey."

She dropped her pencil in surprise. "Sorry, I didn't see you there." She clutched her heart and looked up, her eyes unusually bright. She wore jeans and a t-shirt, what she always wore to work. Her office was unnaturally cold, so I suspected that was why she never wore dresses or skirts.

"Didn't mean to scare you, sweetheart." I walked further inside her office and placed my hands in the pockets of my suit. Whenever I was dressed like this, she paid more attention to me. I suspected she liked the way my body filled it out, my shoulders broad and my chest powerful.

"You're fine." Like never before, she rose from behind her desk and came toward me. Normally, she remained in her chair and just stared at me. But now she was going out of her way to give me affection.

I hoped it would be a kiss this time.

She wrapped her arms around my waist and moved into my body, her face pressed against my chest. She was wearing flats, so she was shorter than usual.

I held her against me and rested my chin on her head. She was the perfect height and shape to fit within my arms. If I could hold her forever, I would. My heart beat at a certain pace just for her, so slow that it might stop altogether. She was a tide of peace that washed over me.

"How are you?"

"Good," she whispered. "You?"

"Really good—now that you're here."

I grinned from ear-to-ear. "Can I take you to lunch?"

"Please."

I grabbed her hand and guided her out of the office. "What are you in the mood for?"

"Anything but pizza."

"What do you have against pizza?"

"I had it last night."

"How about sandwiches?" We were right outside a sandwich shop anyway.

"I could go for a sandwich."

We ordered our food then sat at a table near the window. She took small bites of her sandwich, barely eating anything even though she was hungry. She ate unnaturally slow for a person, and I suspected that was why she was so thin.

Now that our relationship was different I didn't feel guilty for staring at her. I did it when I wanted and however long I wanted. My eyes were glued to her face and I spotted the miniscule freckle in the corner of her mouth. No matter how many times I looked at her, I always spotted something new. The feature I was most obsessed with her were lips. They were full and curved, and I desperately wanted to feel them against my mouth. I'd give anything to kiss her—just once.

When she realized I was staring at her, she met my gaze. Instead of looking awkward or uncomfortable like she used to, she stole a chip from my bag and ate it. She was at ease around me, basking in my attention.

"Have you thought about coming with me to the wedding?" I wanted her by my side the entire time. France was a beautiful place, innately romantic. Maybe our relationship would pick up and progress. Maybe being in a new place would give her a fresh start.

"Yeah."

"And what have you decided?" If she said no, I wouldn't be able to hide my disappointment. I was looking forward to this trip, eating cheese and drinking wine. She would only say no if she wasn't comfortable with me, and I hoped that wasn't the case. Up to this point I've been able to hide my sadness when I didn't get my way. But I wasn't sure if I could do it anymore.

"I'd love to go—if you'll have me."

I couldn't stop the smile from stretching across my face. "I'll always have you."

***

Saturday

It was nine in the evening on a Wednesday and I was standing in front of her door. No matter what I did I couldn't get to sleep despite the fact I had a long day tomorrow. I tossed and turned and found myself wide-awake.

Perhaps Rose could help me.

She opened the door, clearly not expecting to see me at this time of night. She was ready for bed, wearing pajama shorts with a t-shirt. Her hair was in a messy bun and her face was free of makeup. But she made the look sexy. "Hey. Is everything alright?"

"Everything is fine." I didn't walk inside like I normally would. This behavior should be okay, but I didn't want to push my luck. "I'm having a hard time sleeping. I have an early day tomorrow but nothing I do puts me out. I was hoping I could crash here. I always sleep well when I'm with you."

All the anxiety left her face when I finished speaking. "Of course."

I walked inside, glad I was getting my way. At some point in time, I expected her to take a step back from our relationship, to get freaked out over how close we'd become. But thankfully, that didn't happen. She was in this for the long haul.

And so was I.

We went into her bedroom just as we did last time, and once my clothes were off we cuddled together under the covers. I spooned her from behind, my arm tucked tightly around her waist. My face rested against the back of her neck, inhaling her scent like a drug. The second I was in position, I was comfortable. I was in a peaceful place, where nothing could bother me.

"Kyle?"

"Sweetheart?"

"Is there anything I need for the wedding?"

"Nothing but your dancing shoes." My lips moved brushed past her skin as they moved.

"You'll dance with me?" The smile was in her voice.

"Yes. And I'm an amazing dancer."

"Really?"

"Oh yeah."

"I look forward to it."

I tightened my arm and took a deep breath, inhaling her scent.

"Will your whole family be there?"

"Just my mother and I, along with a few close friends." Both of my parents had been only children, and my grandparents were gone. So, my family had always been small.

"Your sister isn't coming?"

I tried not to tense at her question. My sister had been gone for years now and I had enough time to heal, but whenever people asked about her, I dreaded telling the story. It was heartbreaking—to me and everyone else. "No...she's not." I was still on the fence about telling Rose the truth. A part of me thought it would be a good thing. Rose would know that I'd been through something similar, that I understand exactly what she had been through. But then another part of me feared it would make her push me away. "My sister passed away a few years ago."

"Oh..." She stopped breathing, letting my words echo.

I waited for the questions that were bound to come.

"I'm sorry...I didn't know."

"It's okay. It was a long time ago."

"What happened to her?"

It was the moment of truth. "She was walking home late one night in the city. Some guy snatched her, raped her, and then killed her." Whenever I retold the story I forced myself to think about something else. In that moment, I was thinking of the huge cucumbers she would grow in her garden. She refused to tell Mom and me what her secret was.

Rose's entire body stiffened in panic when she heard the terrible tale. Her breathing increased rapidly, going from calm to distressed.

Now I wasn't sure if telling her the truth was wise.

She turned around and faced me, the sadness heavy in her eyes. They were already coated with tears, her reaction immediate. She gave me the biggest look of pity in the world, like her heart just shattered in her chest. "Oh my god…" Her hand moved to my chest in an attempt to comfort me.

"It was hard for all of us. My dad passed away shortly after the trial. The doctors said it was a heart attack that took him, but I think it was a broken heart. He was devastated."

"I can imagine…"

"Thankfully, the guy is sitting in jail for a life sentence. Now he can't hurt anyone else."

She stared at her hand as it rested on mine.

Now was the time for her to tell me the truth. I told her one of my darkest secrets, something that she experienced as well. I knew better than anyone what she had to go through and I wished she would confide in me. Rose was lucky enough to escape with her life. My sister wasn't. Despite all the painful things she experienced, that was one thing she should be grateful for.

But she was silent.

Her eyes were glued to my chest and she breathed quietly, her face covered in a mask of pain. Her fingers dug into my chest gently, like she was reliving the past behind her eyes.

"Sweetheart, are you okay?" We'd reached new levels of this relationship, and I felt entitled to the truth. I wanted her to trust me— completely. I wanted her to know that the past wouldn't change our future.

But she still kept the secret to herself.

I tried not to be disappointed. I had no right to be since I'd never experienced anything like that first hand. But I wished she would see the significance. Before I knew about her past, I felt a distinct connection. It happened the moment I laid eyes on her. And the moment I found out the truth I knew it wasn't a coincidence. We both experienced severe hardships. And that brought us closer together.

I just wish she would realize that.

"I'm so sorry..."

"It's okay." I kept the disappointment out of my voice. She wasn't going to confide in me, and I had to let that go. "It was a long time ago."

"But that's still so devastating..."

"It was. It is." My sister and I weren't particularly close, but we loved each other like all siblings did. She was a beautiful person, on the inside as well as the outside. And she was the spitting image of our mother. Not a day went by when I didn't think about her. "But we have to be strong and move on. If we focus too much on it, we'll become crippled. I know my sister wouldn't have wanted that. We would want to treasure her memory and smile every time we thought about her, not imagine the brutal way she died."

She nodded.

"And putting her murderer behind bars gave my family some closure. It doesn't erase what happened or bring my sister back, but it gave us some sort of satisfaction."

She rubbed my chest gently, trying to comfort me.

And I'd put her assailant behind bars as well.

Saturday

Rose pressed her forehead to mine then ran her fingers through my hair. She felt the soft strands gently, her eyes looking into mine. The sorrow burned from deep within her soul. She felt the same pain I did, carrying it as a burden so I wouldn't carry it alone.

Her fingers slowly drifted down my cheek until they reached my jawline. She felt the stubble that started to come in immediately after I shaved. She felt each strand like she wanted to memorize it, to treasure it.

Her hand migrated to my chin. She felt the stubble there as well as the skin just below my bottom lip. Her eyes were glued to my mouth, appreciating it just the way I appreciated hers.

My body stiffened in anticipation.

She cupped my cheek in a loving way and moved in slightly, her lips almost touching mine.

It took all my willpower to remain still, to keep my hands and lips to myself. I wanted this, more than I could ever explain in words. My body was hot on fire and my heart was about to give out.

Rose crossed the last few inches and slowly pressed her mouth to mine.

Wow.

E. L. Todd

Her lips remained idle, sitting against mine. They were plump and firm, everything I suspected they would be. I could feel the softness of her skin, and when her deep breath fell on my upper lip my dick became hard.

I wished it wouldn't.

Rose kept her mouth there, breathing hard and growing accustomed to the burn between our lips.

I'd never felt this sensation in my life. When I kissed other women, I felt a spark that ignited into a fire. But with Rose, it was an inferno the moment we touched. My fingers sizzled, and my heart skipped a beat every few seconds. The kiss was sexless and practically PG but it was so sexy at the same time.

I couldn't believe she kissed me.

She breathed into my mouth, her bottom lip trembling slightly. I could feel her hesitation as well as her desire. She wanted to kiss me more, kiss me harder.

And I hoped she would.

It took all my strength to not seize control of the moment and suck her lips until they were puckered in red. Naturally, I wanted to roll her to her back and kiss her hard, kiss her everywhere.

305

I wanted to take charge of the moment and kiss her until her lips were chapped.

Somehow, I restrained myself.

Rose gently pulled away, our wet lips slowly breaking apart. The ecstasy was in her eyes, the same kind in mine. Her fingers slowly trailed down my cheek until they moved to my chest. Her breathing was still haywire.

I didn't want it to end. I wanted to keep going and never stop.

Her fingers were digging into my chest, nearly breaking the skin, but she didn't seem to notice. Her eyes were still glued to my lips, as if she couldn't believe what she just did.

I wanted to move in and keep going, but I didn't want to pressure her.

She loosened her grip on my chest when she realized what she was doing. She quickly pulled it away, apologetic for hurting me.

My cock was rock-hard and unable to be subdued. That kiss brought it to life, made it crave something it hadn't had in a long time. It desperately wanted Rose, to be inside her and never leave. I couldn't just make it go away with a simple command. It would take several minutes, maybe an hour, for it to finally deflate.

Rose moved away from me slightly, putting space in between us again.

I didn't want distance. I wanted our bodies to be so close together they formed a single entity. "I want to keep kissing you." I had to train my body to do things differently. Instead of doing what I wanted I had to ask her permission first. Sometimes my desire blocked out all my logic and I turned into a carnal man in desperate need of affection. But I had to keep in mind how different this situation was. I couldn't afford to take one wrong step.

With her breathing still irregular, she stared at my lips.

I held myself back, waiting for her consent.

"I...I'm sorry." She started to move further away, getting out of the bed altogether.

"Sweetheart, that's fine." I grabbed her wrist and steadied her. "Please don't go."

She sat at the edge of the bed, her wrist still clamped tightly in my fingers.

"Come back." I didn't pull her in any direction. My fingers were just loose enough that she could pull away if she wanted to.

She turned back to me, the hesitance in her eyes. "I'm sorry...I'm not trying to lead you on or yank your chain—"

"It's okay. Really." I gently pulled her toward me, making her glide back into bed. "If you ever want to kiss me again, go for it. But if you don't want to, that's fine too."

She tucked her hair behind her ear and avoided eye contact with me. "Maybe this won't work—"

"It will work." I wasn't letting go. "Just relax." I released her altogether and got back into bed. I lay back and remained calm, wanting her to do the same. I rested one arm behind my head and breathed normally.

She got back into bed a moment later, pulling the sheets over her body.

I loved that kiss so much that I couldn't regret it. But if it drove her away, I'd have no other choice but to resent it.

"You must be frustrated with me. If you want to leave and be with someone else, I wouldn't hold it against you."

There was no one else in the world that compared to her. I moved next to her and wrapped my arms around her, making sure she couldn't slip from my grasp. "I'm only frustrated when you push me away. Don't say things like that. I don't want anyone else but you."

"But—"

"I don't want anyone else but you." I'd say it as many times as she needed to hear it. "Now let's go to sleep. I don't know about you, but I have a long day tomorrow." I spooned her from behind and kept my hips slightly out, not wanting her to feel the hard definition in my boxers. It would be unfair for her to hold that against me, something out of my control, but I kept it far away from her and avoided the problem altogether.

Saturday

CHAPTER TWENTY

Rose

When I kissed Kyle, I wasn't thinking. The pull came over me, and my body leaned forward without thinking. A desire burned deep inside me, and the pain from his revelation hit me square in the chest. I wanted to comfort him.

I wanted to comfort myself.

That kiss sent me high into the sky—to the universe. It was powerful and earthshattering. I couldn't keep my feet on the ground for even a second. My lips were so hot they burned, and the rest of my body ached in the same way. It was the first time I wanted to be with a man.

The kiss wasn't the problem. The definition of his hard-on in his boxers wasn't the problem ether.

I was the problem.

Saturday

Could I be with him without telling him the truth? Would that be right? I had the perfect opportunity that night. His sister experienced the same nightmare I did. We shared a common experience. Of all people, he would understand.

But I still couldn't do it.

Would he look at me the same? Would he be so turned off that he would walk away? Would he stay with me just out of pity?

I didn't know what to do. So I ended the embrace and turned away.

Kyle was unbelievably patient with me. He was practically a monk. For a man who could get anyone he wanted, he seemed intent on waiting it out with me. I knew he must be frustrated, being with the same woman for months without getting any action.

But he never complained.

He was making me fall hard for him, getting to the point where I couldn't stand the possibility of losing him. He made me happy in a way no one else ever had. Sometimes I wondered if it was all a dream.

One that I never wanted to end.

It was tense for the following week, and the plane ride to France was also awkward. Kyle didn't bring up that night or try to kiss me again, unless it was on the forehead. He was still affectionate with me like he always was, holding my hand or gripping my waist, but he wasn't quite the same.

I wasn't sure if I should say something.

When we arrived in Cannes, I couldn't believe how beautiful it was. It was right next to the water, the coastline absolutely gorgeous. The sand was pristine white, and all the people were beautiful. Our hotel was right on the water, and it smelled like a scent I'd never experienced. The air was clean and the people were a little brash, but I loved it there all the same.

Kyle checked in. "I have two rooms—both under Kyle."

He had two rooms?

The concierge pulled up the information on the computer. "Yes, I have you down for two suites."

We weren't sharing the same room?

"Thank you." Kyle took the sets of keys then turned to me. "They're right next to each other."

"We aren't staying together...?" I took the card with a shaky hand.

Kyle placed his in his wallet. "I just thought you'd be more comfortable alone."

Saturday

We hadn't slept together since that night with the broken kiss, but I assumed we'd be attached at the hip for the weekend. "Uh...I'd rather stay with you." I missed his strong body keeping me warm. His body heat naturally acted as a heater, keeping the cold sheets comfortable at all times. I loved feeling his powerful body beside mine, like nothing could hurt me when he was near.

"You're sure?"

I nodded.

Kyle watched my face for hesitance, and when he didn't find it he returned the keys to the extra room. "Never mind. We won't be needing these."

**

Kyle hung up his suit in the closet then checked his phone for messages.

"What's the plans for tonight?"

"The rehearsal dinner. The restaurant is right down the road."

"What should I wear?"

"Something fancy." When he finished checking his messages he looked me in the eye. "My mom and Charles have expensive taste."

I opened my suitcase and searched through my outfits, unsure what I should try.

He came to my side then sorted through the dresses. He pulled out a deep blue one that had a low cut in the front. He whistled loudly. "Damn. This is the winner."

I chuckled. "It's not too slutty?"

"Sweetheart, there's no such thing as too slutty."

"There is when I'm meeting your mother for the first time."

"Don't worry about it. You could show up naked and she would still love you."

"Why do I doubt that...?"

"Trust me. She's just happy that I'm happy."

I hadn't met a boyfriend's mother before, but I wasn't nervous to do it for the first time. If she was anything like her son she was wonderful. And since the last woman left Kyle to go back to her ex, I would probably be immediately liked in comparison. "Then this should be easy."

"It'll be a walk in the park, sweetheart."

***

Kyle held my hand as we walked down the narrow sidewalk together. Everything in France was reduced. The roads were thinner, the walkways were slimmer, and even the bathrooms were smaller.

"I'm starving." He dropped my hand and hooked his arm around my waist. His hand rested on my lower back, squeezing the fabric slightly. "How about you?"

"I feel like I'm always hungry."

He chuckled. "Good. You have great metabolism."

"I think I just like to eat."

"That makes two of us." He approached the entrance to the restaurant and held the door open for me.

"Wait." I grabbed his wrist and pulled him off to the side.

"What's up, sweetheart?"

"How should I address your mother?" By her married last name? Her first name?

"Carol is fine."

"You're sure?" I couldn't afford to screw this up.

"Yes." A slow smile crept into his lips. "Where did these nerves come from?"

"I guess I just want this to go well..."

"Sweetheart, you'll be fine. My mother already loves you, as I've told you. The man she's marrying is Charles. He's very nice too. Honestly, you couldn't ask for better people. I know I'm

E. L. Todd

biased and everything, they're down to earth people."

That made me feel a little better. "Okay."

He kissed my forehead before he pulled me inside. "Now let's eat."

***

Kyle's mom was exactly how he depicted her. She was warm and inviting, and she loved Kyle with every fiber of her being. Despite the pain deep in her eyes from losing a husband and a child, she still had a zest for life. She drank more wine than anyone else, and she laughed more than all of us combined.

"So, you're an architect?" Charles asked. "That's very interesting."

"Yes, I enjoy it." I already finished my food and now I was sipping my wine. "It can be stressful sometimes, but I love all the bad moments as well as the good ones."

"I can imagine," he said. "Kyle said you're designing his beach house?"

"I was...I haven't really gotten around to it." I dropped the project when we started dating. I spent all my free time with him so I didn't have a chance to work on his new home.

"Because you've been busy, I hope." Carol smiled before she took a drink. "You have no idea

317

how happy I am that you're here. My son talks about you so much, and it's so nice to finally put a name to a face."

"Mom, chill." Kyle spoke politely, but his tone hinted at his irritation.

"I'm so flattered I was invited. France is so beautiful." This dinner was going way better than I imagined it would. Even though I just met Carol and her fiancée, I felt like I knew them for my entire life.

"Nervous about tomorrow?" Kyle didn't seem to care for the answer, but he was eager to change the subject.

"Not really," Carol said. "Charles and I have been together for a long time. I think it's time we tie each other down."

Charles gave her an affectionate look. "I couldn't agree more."

"Will your kids be there tomorrow?" Kyle asked.

The previous smile on his face evaporated immediately. "No, unfortunately. My kids aren't as open to the idea of me getting remarried as you are."

That was heartbreaking.

"I'm sorry," Kyle said. "For what it's worth, I'm very happy you're getting married."

E. L. Todd

"Thanks, kid," Charles said with a forced smile.

"We aren't going to let them bother us," Carol said. "We make each other happy and that's all that matters. I don't want Charles' money and I don't need it. And he's been alone for almost fifteen years. He deserves to have someone, as do I."

I couldn't agree more.

"You're right, Mom." Kyle clanked his glass against his mother's. "I'll drink to that." He downed the rest of his wine like it was a shot.

I did the same.

"Well, we should get to bed," Charles said. "We have a long day tomorrow."

"You guys better be sleeping in different rooms," Kyle warned. "No hanky-panky the night before the wedding." He shook his forefinger at both of them.

Carol chuckled. "Kyle..."

"I'm being serious," Kyle said. "That's not traditional."

"I think it's okay since we've already been married," Carol said.

"And I need to have the talk with you." He pointed at Charles.

"What talk?" Charles asked.

Saturday

"You know, are you going to treat my mom right? Stuff like that. I'm the man of this family and it's my duty." Kyle smiled so they both knew he was joking.

Charles turned to Carol. "Damn, he's strict."

"He's just protective of me." Her eyes lit up when she looked at her son. "He's a momma's boy."

"Yep." Kyle raised his fist in the air. "And I'm proud of it."

Kyle wasn't just good-looking and successful. He was the biggest sweetheart in the world. He always made everyone around him smile. Making other people happy seemed to bring him the most joy.

"Do we need to have the birds and the bees talk too?" Kyle asked.

Charles chuckled. "I've already had three kids. I think I'm okay."

"Alright," Kyle said. "My door is always open if you need to talk."

Charles turned to me. "You have a good man on your hands, Rose."

"I know." I felt Kyle stare at the side of my face. "I'm very lucky. I'm not sure what I did to deserve such a wonderful man, but I'm not going to think about it too hard. I'm just glad he's mine."

***

"What'd you think?" Kyle kicked off his shoes then undressed himself. He removed his jacket then undid his tie, giving me a private strip show.

"About what?" I slipped off my heels and felt my feet scream in relief.

"About my mom."

"She was great."

"I'm glad the two of you got along." He undid the buttons of his shirt then pulled it off. He returned it to the hanger and let it rest on the back of the chair. "My mom is pretty cool. I don't know very many people who dislike her."

"I doubt anyone dislikes her."

He pulled off his socks then removed his slacks.

I'd seen him nearly naked many times, and I was never ready for the sight. He was undeniably beautiful, fit and strong. He had the body of a Greek god and the heart of a saint. He was the sexiest man I'd ever laid eyes on. Sometimes I couldn't believe I didn't jump on top of him and had my way with him. Whenever we were together, I didn't think about my past. All I thought about was him.

Kyle caught my stare. "Checking me out?" He grinned from ear-to-ear.

"Uh..." I was caught red-handed. "I just..."

"I'll take that as an omission of guilt."

I turned away and stared at my shoes on the ground. I fidgeted with the necklace I wore, trying to find something to do with my hands. My cheeks were turning bright red. I could feel the heat.

Kyle grabbed a bottle of water from the mini-fridge then got into bed. "Are you going to join me anytime soon?" He turned off the lamp and got comfortable.

"Yeah...just let me change." I walked into the bathroom and undressed myself. There was an unusual sensation in my fingertips, a burn that wouldn't die out. My entire body felt hot, and the area between my legs was wet. I hadn't been turned on like this in so long I almost didn't recognize it.

I put on my pajamas but felt awkward doing it. I wanted to walk out there in just my underwear. I wanted to slip under the covers and feel his naked body rub against mine. Instead of sleeping, I wanted to do scandalous things.

Was I ready for it?

I pulled off my pajamas as quickly as I put them on. In just my panties and bra, I looked at myself in the mirror. My makeup was still on and it wasn't smeared. My hair looked pretty decent too. I couldn't believe what I was about to do, but I would regret it if I didn't.

I left the bathroom and walked to the bed. Kyle lay on his back with his eyes closed. His chest rose and fell gently, his breathing calm. The sheets were bunched around his waist, showing his hard chest and defined stomach.

I swallowed the lump in my throat before I slid into the bed beside him. My bare skin rubbed against his, and when he noticed the lack of clothes his eyes opened.

He looked at me with surprise, his eyes immediately moving to my bra and stomach. Instead of touching me, he kept staring. He slowly sat up and his eyes traveled up my body until they met mine.

I couldn't breathe.

"I hope this isn't just to torture me." He leaned down and pressed a kiss to my bare shoulder. He'd never kissed me there before.

It was the greatest sensation I've ever felt in my life.

He pulled his lips away, his eyes hungry for me. "What do you want, sweetheart?"

I swallowed the lump in my throat.

"Tell me. I don't want to misread you." He restrained himself from touching me again. His eyes were on me, eating me alive. But his hands remained stationary.

"I...I want to kiss you."

"What else?"

I wasn't sure.

"Sweetheart."

"I want to be naked with you."

His breathing picked up, and he couldn't hide the desire on his face.

"But I don't want to do more than that..." In the moment I might feel differently, but at that moment I wasn't ready for it.

"Okay." He moved in to kiss me again.

"Even if I say otherwise, I don't want to."

He paused before his mouth touched mine. "That's fine. Even if you beg me it won't happen."

I knew he would respect my wishes even if he wanted more. I could trust him.

He wrapped his arm around me aggressively and dragged me underneath him. He pulled me with such intensity I felt like a log and he was a caveman. He moved on top of me, his stomach next to mine.

Now I couldn't breathe fast enough.

"You can trust me, Rose." He kissed the corner of my mouth before he slowly made his way down my neck. His lips enjoyed me everywhere, tasting the skin of my neck and my chest. He didn't remove what was left of my clothing, choosing to go around it.

When he reached my stomach he pressed light kisses everywhere. He even licked my belly button, something I had no idea could be sexy. Then he moved to the skin of my hips, kissing the fabric of my thong without removing it.

Kyle positioned my leg over his shoulder and kissed my inner thigh.

My nails immediately dug into the sheets and I held back a moan. I never knew my thigh could be such an erogenous zone. My body became ten degrees warmer, and sweat formed on the back of my neck.

He kissed the other thigh, his facial hair brushing up against the skin as he moved. Having a man kiss me like this was the sexiest thing in the world. His mouth glided back up my body until he was positioned above me again.

Saturday

I stared at his chest and noted the hard lines that bisected it everywhere. He was a model for the male anatomy, and I could see every distinction within his body. With minds of their own, my hands moved up his chest and stomach.

Then I wrapped my legs around his waist.

I was surprised by my own actions, but that didn't stop me from doing it. I could feel the definition of his cock through his boxers. He pressed right against my clit, providing just the right amount of friction.

It felt amazing.

Kyle rocked into me slowly, seeing the satisfaction I was getting from it. He brushed his lips passed mine in a tantalizing way, and then he pressed his entire mouth against mine.

My hands trailed to his arms and I dug my fingers into the skin. A moan emerged from the back of my throat, untamed.

His lips didn't move once they were against mine. They just stayed there, hovering. And then he slowly kissed me. He sucked my bottom lip before he massaged my mouth again. He took his time, giving me kisses that were purposeful and sexy.

Wow.

He turned his head slightly to the left, getting more access to my mouth. And then his tongue moved inside, lightly touching mine.

I tightened my thighs around his waist.

He rubbed against me slowly, his cock doing amazing things to my clitoris. I hadn't had this kind of touch in years so my threshold was dangerously low. "I think I'm going to come." I was embarrassed the second I said that. It was a stupid thing to say, but I wasn't thinking when it slipped out. We barely began to fool around and I was going to crumble. He would think it was pathetic.

He spoke into my mouth, still partially kissing me. "Me too."

I wasn't thinking about anything but him. All I could feel was his mouth against mine, the taste of his soft lips. The area between my legs never felt so good. I was on fire, burning in every good way imaginable.

His hand snaked around my back and he unhooked my bra, letting the straps come loose. He gently pulled the material away until my tits were in his view.

He stared at them as he continued to rock. Then he leaned down and kissed the valley between my breasts, kissing and licking the area.

He brought each nipple into his mouth and sucked them aggressively, giving me a twinge of pain that actually felt good.

My hands explored his body further, dragging down his back and feeling the ripple of his muscles. His arms were pinned to either side of me, and I could feel his hot skin as we moved together.

He leaned back and rested on the balls of his feet and his hands moved to the top of my thong. He fingered it gently as he looked me in the eye, making sure I was okay with what was about to happen.

I grabbed his wrists and guided them down my thighs, pulling my underwear with them.

He pulled them off my legs then tossed them on the ground beside the bed. I could feel the moisture between my legs so I knew those panties were soaked. He probably realized it too.

My courage stemmed from an unknown place, and I sat up and grabbed the top of his boxers. I fingered the material for a moment before I slowly pulled them down. Just before his tip popped out I remained still, trying to catch my breath and prepare for what I was about to witness.

Kyle grabbed my wrists just the way I grabbed his earlier and pulled them down, letting his long cock pop out and point directly at me. He was long and thick, enormous and impressive.

"Oh my god…" I kept saying stupid things and I wish I would stop.

He pulled his boxers off and dropped them on top of my panties.

His size threw me off and I couldn't recover. It was a good thing, but it was also a bad thing. My past started to creep back into my thoughts, and I remembered how much it hurt. It was rough and violent, and I cried through the entire ordeal.

Kyle knew my mind had drifted. He wrapped his hand around my neck and forced me to look directly at him. "Stay with me."

I looked him in the eye and felt the past fade away.

He moved on top of me and separated my legs. It seemed like he was positioning himself to be inside me, but he said that wouldn't happen tonight. And if that's what he said, then he meant it.

He pressed a soft kiss to my lips before he spoke. "It's just you and me, sweetheart."

"I know…" It surprised me how sensitive he was. He had no idea what happened to me, but he was still unnaturally thoughtful to my feelings and emotions. He never asked me where my hesitance came from, and he gave me the patience I needed. He was an incredible man—the most incredible.

He pressed his cock directly against my folds, the area between my legs that was throbbing so much it hurt. I was slick down below, flooded with moisture that he elicited. A quiet moan rumbled from deep in the back of his throat. "You're so wet for me."

So wet it was a little embarrassing. At least he enjoyed it. I cupped his face and felt his cock slide back and forth. Every time he moved against my clitoris it felt so amazing. My back was arching and my body was tightening. I felt the distant burn deep inside my core. It was slowly building, about to erupt into a crescendo.

I tried to fight the moans that escaped my lips, but more kept coming, and more often. "Oh god…" Nothing had ever felt this good in my life. Just feeling him rub against me sent my body into overdrive. I couldn't handle everything he was giving me. It felt so good it hurt.

"Sweetheart..." That same rumble erupted from the back of his throat. His arms were tightening, showing the distinction of muscles and veins. His back was tight from his thrusts.

I couldn't believe it was happening. I was about to spiral head first into a world of pleasure. Years had come and gone and I hadn't experienced a single one in that amount of time. But now I was on the brink of the best one I've ever had.

It hit me the same way lightning strikes the earth. The collision was so powerful it shook the earth, affecting everything within its radius. The soil was burning hot, still smoking.

And that's exactly how I felt.

My head rolled back and I dug my fingers into his arms, feeling the blinding sensation between my legs. I screamed for the entire duration, but I was so blind-sided, I wasn't sure what was happening.

He continued to rub against me before he released a deep moan. Then he exploded onto my stomach, still pumping into me as he released every drop.

Seeing him release onto my skin was sexy enough to make my orgasm last a little longer. My body ached in a grateful way, pleased that I had an experience I'd denied myself for so long.

Kyle looked down at me, the same pleased look on his face. His eyes were heavy with sleep and he seemed satisfied, just as satisfied as I was. He leaned down and pressed a kiss to my sweaty forehead, his chest still racing with his deep breathing.

"That felt so good..."

"I'm glad you liked it." He grabbed the box of tissues on the nightstand and wiped away his seed on my stomach. Then he cleaned himself off, removing all the thick, white drops.

It was a lot.

He tossed everything on the ground then lay beside me on the bed. Instead of waiting for me to come to him like he usually did, he grabbed me and positioned me on his chest, exactly where he liked me. His arms rested on my lower back and he closed his eyes, ready for sleep.

Even though we were both still sweaty, I didn't mind. I listened to his deep breaths, feeling the rise and fall of his chest. It was a lullaby to me, a song that made me relax.

It was difficult to keep my eyes open when the exhaustion crept in. That orgasm knocked the wind out of me, sucking away all my energy. I never knew an orgasm could feel that good.

It felt like the first one I ever had.

***

Kyle walked his mom down the aisle, wearing a deep navy blue suit. His eyes were on his mother's face the entire time, watching her smile light up the world around her. When he handed her over to Charles, he winked at him. "I know you'll take care of her."

Charles smiled then pulled Carol in front of the pastor.

Only thirty people were at the ceremony on the beach. It was held at a private estate, property Charles had owned for several years. The weather was beautiful and the wind was absent on the beach.

It couldn't have been a more perfect day.

Kyle took the seat beside me and held my hand. "How'd I do?"

"Great."

"I look sexy in my suit, huh?" He wiggled his eyebrows.

"I'm not sure how I can keep my hands off you for the rest of the evening."

His teasing nature disappeared, and now he looked nothing but serious. "Then don't."

Saturday

Kyle and I sat together at the dinner table, enjoying the prime rib and delectable wine they had. Platters of cheese and bread were on every table, and it was definitely the best I'd ever had.

Carol and Charles were dancing together under the stream of white lights. The ocean was in the background, and the sunset over the horizon. It was dusk, and the sky couldn't look more beautiful.

"Can I have this dance?" Kyle extended his hand.

"Should we give them the floor?"

"No. Mom specifically told me she wanted to see us dance at her wedding. It's her gift."

I placed my hand in his and allowed him to pull me into the center of the dance floor. He took up a proper position and slowly danced with me, guiding me every step of the way.

Carol looked over at us, and she smiled so genuinely it seemed like she might cry.

"Your mother cares about your happiness more than her own."

"That's true. She told me I better give her grandchildren before she dies."

"And will you?"

"Absolutely."

I pictured me and him expecting our first child. I was swollen and pregnant, and Kyle was opening every door and waiting on me hand-and-foot. His mother and Charles would be at the hospital when I delivered, and I could picture their smiling faces right then and there.

He brought me closer into his chest as he moved, his eyes soaking me in. "Last night was fun."

Neither one of us had mentioned it until now. "It was…"

"Every time I think about it, I get hard."

Those words made me hard myself.

"I'm having a great time tonight, but I'm eager to go back to the room."

Last night I did a lot of things I wasn't sure I could do. I kissed a man, our bodies completely naked, and we did sexual things that were more satisfying than any other sexual experience I'd ever had. I didn't think I could get to this point, but Kyle brought me there.

I knew I needed to tell him the truth. Last night shouldn't have happened without everything out in the open. It was my business and my past, but I felt deceitful hiding it from him. Deep down inside, I still didn't want to tell him.

Saturday

I was afraid I would lose him.

Now that I'd fallen so hard for him I wasn't sure if I could walk away. Kyle had become such an intricate part of my life. He pulled all my walls down and showed me how to trust again. Not all the men in the world were evil—only a few.

"You look great in that dress—but I think it'd look better on my hotel floor."

The cheesy line made me smile. "Does that line usually work?"

"It worked on you, didn't it?" He wiggled his eyebrows playfully.

I chuckled and kept dancing with him, loving the way he cradled me as we moved. He gripped me tightly but with just the right amount of softness. His lips brushed passed mine every few minutes, teasing me. "Thank you for taking me along."

"There's no one else I'd rather share this moment with." He turned me slightly, passing his mom. She gave us a smile before she kept dancing. "And I don't think anyone else would have made my mom happier."

I smiled and felt the redness in my cheeks.

"When we get back home, she's going to hammer me about marrying you."

"You think?"

"I know," he said with a laugh. "She thinks I'm old and need to settle down. But she doesn't understand people of our generation aren't getting married young anymore. We take our time and explore the world before we choose a partner. Perhaps I'm picky, but I was waiting for the right girl."

"I don't think that's picky. I think it's romantic."

"Well...I think I have found the right girl." He squeezed my waist as he continued to dance with me. He completely led our direction because I was physically unable to do anything. He watched my reaction, searching my eyes deep down into my soul.

His words were so beautiful they were heartbreaking. The sincerity in his voice washed over me in waves, exciting me and terrifying me at the same time. In my heart, I knew I felt the same way. It was obvious.

But now I had to tell him the truth.

***

When the night ended, it was after midnight. For older people, they sure didn't go to bed early.

"Where are they going on their honeymoon?" I walked inside our room then set my clutch on the table.

"Switzerland."

"That'll be nice."

"Yeah, I'm sure it will." The second he was inside he came up behind me and wrapped his arms around my waist. He pinned me against his chest and kissed my neck, devouring me like I was his.

I couldn't get over how good it felt.

Kyle pulled my hair over one shoulder and continued to kiss me. Then he grabbed my chin and turned my neck toward him, kissing me hard on the mouth and guiding me further into the room. "You looked so beautiful tonight. That was all I could think about."

I gripped his hips behind me, latching onto him. "Not as beautiful as you."

He pulled off his jacket and quickly yanked off his tie. His shirt was gone in a nanosecond then he was back to kissing me. "Now that I can kiss you that's all I want to do."

Now there was no turning back. I'd fallen hard for this man and couldn't picture myself with anyone else. He brought me back to life and he didn't even realize it. He made me whole by putting together all my broken pieces.

So I couldn't make love to him without telling him the truth.

He had the right to know.

"Kyle?"

He stopped kissing me and pressed his lips to my ear. "Sweetheart."

I turned around and faced him head-on. Now I had to look at him I realized how hard this was. It might be the last conversation we ever had. It could be the last moment he would ever look at me like that. All that affection would die away, and nothing but disgust would remain. "There's something I want to tell you."

He turned serious, but his eyes were still hungry for me. He kept his hands to his sides but they shook slightly, like they wanted to grab me by their own will. His obsessive need to touch me was romantic and sexy. No man had ever treated me that way. "I'm listening."

"I didn't want to be with you in the beginning because I just wasn't ready. I didn't want to date any more than I had to, and there was no one I was interested in anyway. But that was before you came along..."

Saturday

His eyes were locked to mine, hanging on to every word I said.

"You've changed my life in so many good ways. Reality became better than my dreams, and I longed to be with you every chance I got. I never thought I could feel that way. I never thought...I could fall in love."

His eyes immediately softened and he looked at me in a new way. Now his look was full of an entirely new emotion altogether. Our relationship had changed irrevocably in that moment and there was no going back.

"And I—"

"I love you too."

My entire body stopped functioning. My heart stopped beating, my lungs cut off my air supply, and even my brain turned off. All I did was feel—feel everything. This incredible man loved me.

He loved me.

Kyle closed the gap between us and cupped my cheeks. His mouth was on mine quicker than I could stop him, and then a beautiful kiss ensued. It was soft and gentle, but it was strong and full of angst. He needed to kiss me because he would die if he stopped.

E. L. Todd

My lips trembled under his touch, and my hands gripped his to hold onto something. The passion and fire between us was enough to burn down everything around us. It was the kind of love I thought only existed in fictional worlds, not real life.

Kyle unzipped my dress as he continued to kiss me, and then he pulled each strap down, letting it snake down my body until it fell to the floor. He unclasped my strapless bra, and when it came loose it thudded softly against the carpet.

The more articles of clothing that fell, the deeper I fell into him. Our kiss became heated and desperate, like we needed each other then and there just to survive.

He grabbed my thong and pulled it down, kissing my hips as he helped me step out of the material. When he rose to his feet again I undid his slacks and pulled them off. He kicked off his shoes then everything else, including his boxers. All that was left were his socks.

He guided me on the bed and moved on top of me, pulling off his socks as he went. His mouth was on mine again, and he kissed me harshly. It was as gentle as it was yesterday, but it somehow felt better.

Saturday

We moved together in our heated embrace, kissing and touching one another. The area between my legs was soaked and ready for his entrance. The past was irrelevant and didn't enter my mind once. All I thought was Kyle and how much I wanted him. I wanted to be with him, to show him just how much I loved him.

He stopped kissing me and separated his legs with mine. He pressed his forehead to mine and breathed deeply, the sweat already on his chest. "Can I make love to you?"

"Yes." The words were out of my mouth before I could even think them. My body wanted him as well as my heart. I knew this was right. I knew Kyle was the right guy to share this moment with. He stole my heart a long time ago, and now I wanted to fall even further into him.

He grabbed a condom and rolled it on his length before he positioned himself over me.

Instead of being afraid I was excited. What we were about to have was beautiful and pleasurable. It would be just like last night, but better. I gripped his arms as I waited for him to enter me.

He pressed his tip inside me and slowly stretched me apart, taking his time and giving me a second to acclimate. I was soaked down below so he was able to move inside easily.

The second I felt him I bit my bottom lip.

He pushed further inside me, stretching me wide as his entire length penetrated me. He moved until he was balls-deep. He studied my face, making sure it felt good.

I ran my hands up his chest and enjoyed his fullness. It didn't hurt in the least. In fact, it felt unbelievably good. He was big for my small size, but my body handled him because I was so aroused.

He kissed my forehead before he slowly rocked into me, giving me gentle thrusts. The pace was irrelevant. He took it slow, enjoying every movement we both felt.

I wrapped my arms around his shoulders and gripped him tightly, holding on as I moved with him. I rocked my hips from below, taking in his length over and over. He never increased his speed, going as slow as possible.

But I liked it that way.

Kyle looked me in the eye as he moved inside me, watching every reaction I felt to him. He seemed to be paying more attention to my enjoyment than his own.

Saturday

I fingered his strands of hair and felt my lips brush past his. I couldn't control my breathing because everything felt so magnificent. It was the first time I had sex that was beautiful and sexy at the same time. Neither one of us cared about getting off. All we cared about was sharing the moment.

"You're okay, sweetheart?" His chest and arms were covered in sweat, making his skin shiny and slippery.

"More than okay."

He positioned my legs over his shoulders then leaned far over me, his head pressed to mine. He gave me the same slow thrusts, but now he went deeper inside me.

It felt too good to be true. "Kyle…"

"You're going to come." He increased his pace slightly. "I can feel it…"

I didn't know how he knew that, but I didn't ask. I dug my nails into his skin as I felt the distant burn I'd recently become familiar with. It flushed through my entire body and made me come alive like a white, hot inferno. My entire body shut down just for a moment to accommodate the feelings.

And then it hit me.

"Oh my god…"

Carnal and aroused, he looked into my eyes with the same expression. Watching me explode around his cock brought him to the same level where I was placed. After a quiet groan, he buried himself as far inside me as he could go and he released.

I pulled him further into me, loving the fact he was experiencing what I just felt a second ago—and I was the one who made him feel that.

He depleted himself entirely before his breathing returned to normal. He kept his body on top of mine like he didn't want to leave anytime soon. "I'm sorry. I could go longer, but my stamina isn't what it used to be."

"It was perfect."

"Yeah?" He kissed me, tasting salty.

"Yeah."

He rubbed his nose against mine, the first time he ever did that with me. "I'm satisfied, but I still want you..."

"I want you too."

"Then I'm not going anywhere." He kissed me again, his embraces soft and gentle. He stayed on top of me and ran his fingers through my hair, loving me with everything he had. Within minutes he grew hard inside me once more, and then he slowly started to rock.

Saturday

Our plane was leaving in the morning, but it didn't seem like we'd get any sleep prior to that. But neither one of us seemed to care. Maybe we would miss our flight altogether. Maybe we would just do this—and never stop.

CHAPTER TWENTY-ONE

Kyle

I was going to tell her the truth.

I swear.

But then she told me she loved me.

And I forgot about everything else.

I knew she was fond of me and we were going somewhere, but I hadn't expected her to say those words out loud. And I didn't expect her to say them at the night of my mother's wedding.

When she did, everything else faded away. I'd spent my whole life looking for the right woman to settle down with. That cliché image, the house with the picket fence, two dogs, and a wife and two kids was exactly what I wanted. I kept trying to force that on Francesca because I loved her, but in the end I realized she wasn't the right one for me.

It was Rose.

Saturday

Now that I'd found her, everything made sense. We may not have a marriage and kids right away, but they would happen someday. She was the person who completed me.

And I couldn't believe my luck that she was so perfect.

We returned from France and got back to our regular lives. Rose had a project to work on, and I was due in court.

The trial was starting.

Now that Rose told me she loved me the trial was even more difficult. I was personally invested in this case, and if I didn't win I'd kill myself. Both Rose and Audrey needed justice, and I was going to make it happen.

"How are you doing?" Mark walked into my office and watched me gather my briefcase. It was early in the morning, too early for everyone else to be there. I was only there because my case started at nine and I had to get my things together.

"I'm ready to nail this piece of shit to the wall. So, I'm great." I pulled the satchel over my shoulder then adjusted my tie. The idea of handcuffing myself to my desk didn't seem like such a bad idea. I wasn't sure if I could stop myself from strangling Peter with my bare hands.

"I hope you've decided to use Rose as a witness." He stood with his hands in his pockets, quickly overstaying his welcome.

"No."

"Kyle, let me sit in on this. I can help you."

"I don't want any help." I didn't need any help.

"I went through this with Rose the first time. I'm a behemoth of information."

"I read all your files, Mark. I appreciate the offer, but I can handle this solo."

Mark bowed his head, deterred.

"I'll get him, alright?" I clapped him on the shoulder before I walked out.

"And I think Rose is the best way to make that happen."

I wasn't bringing her into this. And honestly, I didn't think it would make a difference anyway. It would only remind the jury that he'd been claimed innocent once. I wouldn't want to give them another reason to think he may be innocent. "With all due respect, you lost her case. And I'm going to win this one."

***

The trial began with the opening statements. Since I was the prosecutor, I went first. I paced around the courtroom, in perfect view of the jury. My good looks and nice suit were bound to make an impression on them. But it was my words that would carry the most weight. "Peter Gamble isn't the innocent man you hope he is. He's the kind of man you fear for your daughters. He's a predator, lurking on the Internet under a false name and good looks. Once he snags something in his net, he pulls it in. To make things worse, he charges money for other men to get in on the scheme." I swallowed the lump in my throat because this was becoming more difficult than I anticipated. "Audrey Frank was an innocent woman who thought she was going on a blind date. Instead, she was tied down and raped by four different men. Once they were finished, they beat her until she barely clung onto life. I have the evidence, the testimonies, and the witnesses to prove this man is guilty beyond reasonable doubt. Thank you." I walked back to my seat and took a long drink of water. Audrey sat beside me, her head down and her eyes downcast. I patted her on the shoulder. "I'm going to get him, Audrey. I promise."

***

I was physically and emotionally drained to the point of exhaustion. All I wanted to do was go to bed and never wake up again. It was difficult for me to be in the same room as the man who assaulted the woman I loved.

It was suffocating.

Having to talk about the evidence out loud and recount everything that happened that night was agonizing. These things happened to Audrey, but I knew they also happened to Rose. When I pictured them holding her down and doing these things to her bile came into my mouth.

I wanted to shoot him in the head.

Somehow, I stayed calm and did my best work. There was no one who wanted a conviction more than I did, and I was going to get one if it was the last thing I did.

I'd only been home for thirty minutes when there was a knock on my door.

I knew who it was. "Come in, sweetheart."

Rose walked inside with a bag under her arm. Her smile lit up the room like it usually did. "How'd you know it was me?"

The trial was forgotten the moment I looked at her. "Just a hunch."

She set the bag on the table then wrapped her arms around me, giving me a hug that told me how much she missed me that day. "I brought you dinner. I know you must be tired from working on your case."

"It hasn't been bad." It was easy to lie through my teeth about this since I was protecting her from the truth. "But thank you for dinner." Instead of kissing her forehead the way I used to, I kissed her on the lips. I loved having the liberty to do whatever I wanted, when I wanted. I could take her into the bedroom and have my way with her if that was what I really wanted.

"You're welcome. It was just an excuse to see you anyway."

I dug my hand into her hair and yanked her back slightly, forcing her to look up at me. "You never need to make up an excuse, sweetheart. You can see me whenever you damn well please."

"Yeah? I like that."

I kissed her hard on the mouth and felt my dick immediately spring to life. Now I didn't care about anything else except having her on my bed. I wanted her right then and there—and all night long.

E. L. Todd

CHAPTER TWENTY-TWO

Rose

My life had been put back together by a very special man. Kyle was everything I wanted in another person, and I never thought I could feel this way again. He washed away the taint that stained my body. He removed every impurity, scar, and mark.

I was going to tell him the truth in France, but when I told him I loved him, he said it back. And then I didn't know what to do. The happiness flooded my body and everything else faded to the background. It didn't seem important anymore—at least in that moment.

Now that everything was said and done, I didn't know what to do. Telling him now may not make much of a difference. But I felt guilty for keeping it from him. Months ago he was interested to know why I was so timid when it

353

came to dating. Now that he was my boyfriend he deserved an answer.

But I still dreaded telling him.

***

I was at the office when I got a call from someone I hadn't spoken to in nearly four years.

"Rose Perkins?" The man's voice came over the phone.

"This is she." I still had no idea who this was. Maybe he was a new customer looking to build something.

"This is Mark Robinson."

I remembered his name but couldn't place him. How did I know him? Was he a former client?

"I was your attorney for the trial four years ago..."

"Oh, I'm sorry." I slapped my forehead in embarrassment. I couldn't believe I forgot who he was. "Of course. How are you?"

"Good. You?"

"I'm great. Just working." I paused when I realized I didn't have any idea what he wanted. Why was he calling me? "Can I help you with something?" The trial didn't end the way I wanted. Peter went free, and I changed my apartment and wiped my presence off social media. You couldn't even find my email.

"I just thought you should know Peter is back on trial again. Apparently, he's done the same thing to another woman and there's substantial evidence against him. The lawyer taking the case said he didn't want to involve you in it, but I thought you had the right to know what was going on."

I listened to everything he said, but I couldn't process it. It took a minute for it to soak into my brain. "Wow...I don't know what to say." I was upset he hurt another woman, but I was also grateful he was on the stand again. Maybe this time he would be convicted and put away for the rest of his life. "Thank you for telling me."

"You're welcome. The trial started on Monday and it'll probably last for two weeks. Not sure if you want to sit in on it but you're allowed to."

I didn't want to have anything to do with the new case, but I also felt compelled to go. I had to see him pay for his crimes. I had to see him end up in jail.

I had to. "I'm surprised I wasn't asked to testify." I didn't want to take the stand, but I would do whatever it took to put Peter away.

"The attorney on this case said it was best to leave you out of it."

"Why?"

"Since he was claimed innocent in your trial, he thought it may sway the jury in a bad direction."

"I see…"

"I'm pretty sure he's going down this time, Rose. I have a good feeling about it."

"I hope you're right."

"Well…take care."

"Thank you, Mark." I hung up then stared at the surface of my desk, trying to take in all the information that was just dropped on me. Peter didn't stop even after he was almost put in jail for the rest of his life. The fact he continued the same behavior was absolutely despicable. Even though it wouldn't do me any good I needed to attend that trial.

I needed to watch him burn.

***

I got into my seat just before the trial continued. I was sitting in the third row right at the aisle. Peter and his two lawyers were directly in front of me. He wore an orange jumpsuit with handcuffs on his wrists. I could only see the back of his head, but that small glimpse was enough to confirm it was he.

The victim sat next to her lawyer, her head ducked down and her hair covering her face. She slouched forward, like she wanted to disappear and go unnoticed. Her lawyer wore a charcoal gray suit with dark brown hair. I could only see the back of his head, but he reminded me of someone—someone I couldn't place.

The judge began the proceedings with a short introduction. Then a witness took the stand, a woman about the victim's age.

The lawyer in the charcoal gray suit stood and approached the stand, tall with powerful shoulders. He stood with his hands in his pockets before he started speaking. "You were there that night when Audrey had a date with the defendant, right?"

I recognized that voice.

"Yes," the witness answered.

"You waited on their table, correct?" he asked.

"Yes," she said.

"Was it clear it was a blind date?" he asked.

"Yes," she answered. "They introduced themselves at the beginning, and then they talked about the dating website they met on."

The lawyer turned around and approached the jury, a fierce look in his eyes. He looked maniacal, the exact opposite of the way his voice sounded. I only knew that because I knew him so well.

It was Kyle.

It was so strange I thought it was a dream. How could Kyle be defending Audrey? That would mean he knew about my case and what happened to me.

He knew what happened to me.

I gasped and stood up, unable to believe what my two eyes were telling me. Kyle knew about my past all along. He probably knew the moment we met. He'd been keeping it a secret this entire time.

I couldn't believe it.

Kyle turned my way when the rest of the crowd did. He simply glanced at me in the beginning, but once he realized who I was, he stood frozen to the spot. Panic emerged on his face, and it was clear he wanted to say something, to stop me from leaving without an explanation.

I felt so stupid. I'd felt guilty for not telling him the truth, but he knew the entire time anyway. Now I understood why he was so patient with me, walking on eggshells all the time. Now I understood why he fought for me so hard, knowing I was a rape victim. He used that information to his advantage and manipulated me right where he wanted me to be.

The tears welled up in my eyes and I couldn't stop them. I couldn't look at Kyle for a moment longer and I never wanted to look at him again. I gave him one final look of betrayal before I turned on my heel and left.

And I never looked back.

Saturday

E. L. Todd

I hoped you enjoyed reading SATURDAY as much as I enjoyed writing it. It would mean the world to me if you could leave a short review. It's the best kind of support you can give an author. Thank you so much.

Is that really the end of Kyle and Rose? Or is there still hope? Find out in the next installment of the series SUNDAY.

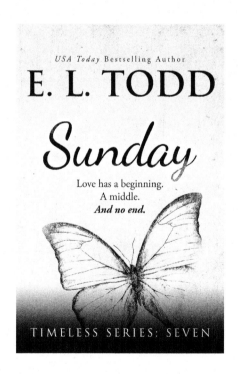

Saturday

Want To Stalk Me?

Subscribe to my newsletter for updates on new releases, giveaways, and for my comical monthly newsletter. You'll get all the dirt you need to know. Sign up today.
www.eltoddbooks.com

Facebook:
https://www.facebook.com/ELTodd42

Twitter:
@E_L_Todd

Now you have no reason not to stalk me. You better get on that.

EL'S Elites

I know I'm lucky enough to have super fans, you know, the kind that would dive off a cliff for you. They have my back through and through. They love my books and they love spreading the word. Their biggest goal is to see me on the New York Times bestsellers list and they'll stop at nothing to make it happen. While it's a lot of work, it's also a lot of fun. What better way to make friendships than to connect with people who love the same thing you do?

Are you one of these super fans?

If so, send a request to join the Facebook group. It's closed so you'll have a hard time finding it without the link. Here it is:

https://www.facebook.com/groups/11923269 20784373/

Hope to see you there, ELITE!

Printed in Great Britain
by Amazon